NIGHT GALLERY

NIGHT GALLERY

Rod Serling

With an Introduction by Scott Skelton and Jim Benson

ROD SERLING BOOKS™

ISBN-13: 9781493716975
ISBN-10: 1493716972

CONTENTS

ROD SERLING'S NIGHT GALLERY

FOREWORD BY SCOTT SKELTON AND JIM BENSON

By the late 1950s, Rod Serling was at the height of his career as a television dramatist but growing increasingly frustrated with one of the harsher realities of the business: censorship. By creating *The Twilight Zone*, he turned from producing topical dramas with controversial themes to writing in the marginally regarded (at the time) genre of science fiction and fantasy. In this way, he could effectively skirt the inevitable meddling of sponsors and television executives too timid to air an unvarnished examination of, say, the Emmett Till murder.

This is not to say that Rod Serling wasn't an enthusiastic devotee of speculative fiction — he most certainly was — but his use of the genre's unconventional settings and themes allowed him to perform a bit of playwriting sleight of hand and slip his social concerns and humanist views past the Powers That Be without their notice. And to our great pleasure, it allowed Serling to do what he did best: spin some fantastically diverting yarns.

As curator and host of his second anthology TV series, *Night Gallery*, Serling took a turn toward horror and the occult, employing as his setting a shadowy museum of macabre paintings and statuary — the sly hook on which to hang his prodigious narrative gifts. "I'm more or less a professional practitioner of art that tells a story," he asserted in one of his introductions, "and stories that dabble in themes that don't lend themselves to dinner conversation."

Indeed not.

"We welcome you to this palladium of art treasures that range from the kooky to the uncommon, from the bestial to the bizarre — a collection of paintings on display for only the most discriminating, because it's best that they be seen both after and *in* the dark." And like those canvases, this collection is best savored late in the evening, with lights turned low and a flickering blaze in the fireplace to drive away the chills.

These six tales, first released in a Bantam paperback collection in November 1971, are prose versions of scripts produced for the brief first season of *Night Gallery*. The settings are as diverse as imagination can devise: a big game hunter's trophy room; the decks of a British ocean liner on a fog-enshrouded North Atlantic crossing; the unforgiving spotlight on the stage of a sleazy, last-chance nightclub; the mourning room of a murderer's home; the deserted, boarded-up haunts of a deeply cherished past; and the blackest, coldest reaches of outer space. If you've ever watched an episode of the series, the characters you meet here may seem familiar — some flawed, some hateful, often desperate or haunted — but with the extra dimension of their inner lives now on the page, their hopes and fears will be brought to light fully by Serling's keen insights into his fellow man.

So, reader ... lower the lights ... set a match to the fireplace logs ... and enjoy your investigation into some of the darker corners of Rod Serling's imagination:

"The name of this place, should you have come in here accidentally out of the rain, is the *Night Gallery*. We deal in paint, pigment, light and shadow — realism, surrealism, impressionism, and ghost stories. And now, tonight's first excursion into the realm of the unusual...."

The Sole Survivor

The tale of the exile trying in vain to return home from the sea is as old as Homer. The poets Samuel Taylor Coleridge and Heinrich Heine added their own twists of sin and redemption to the mythology of the doomed seafarer wandering the seas on an endless voyage. In "The Sole Survivor," Rod Serling takes those threads of tradition and weaves a very twentieth-century twist to the classic tale.

While scripting this episode, he paid scrupulous attention to historical detail, ensuring his dialogue was accurate by contacting an expert in maritime traditions of the period to find the exact orders and responses that would be traded among British naval officers while changing course and retrieving a lifeboat.

Serling's first drafts of this script had some notable differences from the final product, with (in one version) *six* people rescued while drifting in a sea of lost ships. Titled variously "Entries in a Ship's Log," "Object on the Horizon," and finally "The Sole Survivor" on his last draft, the episode was ultimately called "Lone Survivor" — probably for the simple reason that the term "sole survivor" suggests that the rescued individual was the only survivor of the *Titanic* disaster, when history proves there were more than 700 passengers and crew members pulled from the freezing Atlantic waters, victims of that fateful night in April 1912.

Opening Narration

An unforgiving sea usually buries its secrets beneath itself. War ships and ocean liners, treasure galleons and submarines turn into rusting relics inside a watery locker, lost to memory. But occasionally there comes a floating unbidden reminder of disaster — like this lifeboat. The painting is called "The Lone Survivor." We'll put it in tow and see where she came from and why.

Make Me Laugh

Rod Serling's peculiar ability to illuminate the lives of the desperate and misbegotten gets a workout in this tragicomic tale, tapping into the "careful what you wish for" aspect of some of his most popular *Twilight Zone* scenarios as well. Characters like Jackie

Slater are the author's strong suit, and we've seen them more than a few times in his oeuvre — usually long on self-delusion, always short on luck. Slater is "Mountain" McClintock with a stand-up routine, a sweaty-collared has-been who never really was, hungering for respect in a world with zero to give.

Despite the usually inspired directorial hand of a young Steven Spielberg, the production of this *Night Gallery* episode left its author less than impressed. "It's really a piece of crap," Serling beefed. "It almost single-handedly brought back vaudeville." Saddled with a pair of badly miscast players in Godfrey Cambridge and Jackie Vernon, Spielberg was unable to bring out the pathos inherent in the script. The short story, however, is a pleasure, rife with Serling's pungent wit, acute descriptive powers, and flavorful dialogue. The reader can assemble a luxury cast in his or her mind: Jackie Gleason and Sam Jaffe ... Rodney Dangerfield and Vincent Schiavelli ... Quiet on the set ... Lights, camera, *action!*

Opening Narration

On display this evening, a pastiche of paintings from Oddball Land. The poet Sir Max Beerbohm reflected that no one ever died of laughter. Object of brush and palette: the rebuttal. The clown is Jackie Slater — his occupation, a comedian. His aspirations, to collect funny bones and hang them on the walls of his life to hide the cracked plaster and yellowed wallpaper that is part of the interior decoration of failure. Poor Jackie Slater: a bad joke told in a foreign language in an empty hall — the comic unable to coax laughter. The painting is called "Make Me Laugh," and this lightless limbo is called the Night Gallery.

Pamela's Voice

This script was one of Rod Serling's first-season favorites, a two-character study he could sink his teeth into and thoroughly relish: "'Pamela's Voice' is a marvelous tour de force for a performer. It deals with just two people, and gave me a chance to *write* for people." Brief and bitchy, the episode segment stars Phyllis Diller (of the magpie cackle) and John Astin (*The Addams Family*'s Gomez, now gone to seed) as the eternally bickering couple. For my money, Serling's prose version plays even better, caustic and jovially mean-spirited, with no barriers to strong language or limitations on displaying the messy and thoroughly entertaining business of murder.

Opening Narration
Welcome, art lovers. We offer for your approval a still life, if you will, of noise — a soundless canvas suggestive of sound. The mouth belongs to Pamela. In life, a shrieking battle-ax made up of adenoids, tonsils, and sound decibels. In death, an unmuted practitioner of fishwifery, undeterred and ungagged by what one would assume to be the Great Silencer. Some ghosts come back to haunt; others come back simply to pick up where they left off. Our painting is called "Pamela's Voice," and this is the Night Gallery.

Does the Name Grimsby Do Anything to You?

Rod Serling wrote his first submission for the *Night Gallery* series in outline form immediately after NBC bought the series in December 1969. This seems appropriate, since this story acts as a complement to the first script he wrote for *The Twilight Zone* — "Where Is Everybody?" — revisiting themes of isolation and the lurking threat of space madness first examined there.

"Does the Name Grimsby Do Anything to You?" delves into the delicate psyche of an *Apollo* astronaut, driven by his fierce ambition to be the first man to walk on the moon. Presented during the early planning stages for the show, the idea was jettisoned — perhaps for its expense, with its many scenes set in space and on the lunar surface. Perhaps also for the fact that it would have been acknowledged worldwide that Neil Armstrong and Buzz Aldrin had been the first citizens of Earth to set foot on the moon in July 1969. Without some suspension of belief on the audience's part or philosophical musings about some parallel universe in the story's introduction, its effect might have been severely lessened.

Serling developed his outline as the short story that appears here. A vignette of more modest ambitions on the same lunar theme arrived from Serling's pen and was produced for the series, a curious little shocker titled "The Nature of the Enemy." But "Does the Name Grimsby Do Anything to You?" is far richer psychologically, more compelling dramatically, and might have made an outstanding episode of *The Twilight Zone* had Serling written it a decade earlier.

Opening Narration

This offering is a landscape, lunar and low-keyed, suggestive perhaps of some of the question marks that await us in the stars ... and perhaps pointing up the moment when we'll collect something other than moon rocks. This item is called "The Nature of the Enemy."

Clean Kills and Other Trophies

The event that triggered the penning of Rod Serling's fierce polemic against guns, game hunting, and their practice as a measure of manhood was entirely commonplace: an invitation from a neighborhood couple to something called a "safari dinner":

"The host, he's a big hunter. He goes to Africa about two months a year, and he shoots, and he kills, and he does so with gusto and with great pleasure. This is his big thing; some men like girls, other guys like .40 caliber bullets. I'm not suggesting that all men who hunt are, in some strange, sick way, unwell, and I'm sure there's an ecological reason why some herds have to be thinned. But personally I can't stand hunting."

"We arrived at this gentleman's home, and the first thing we saw was a mounted boar's head on the wall, followed by a dead oce-lot, a leopard, a monkey, a rhinoceros, a giraffe — all glassy-eyed, resigned to death, staring at us from the walls. The ashtrays were made out of the feet of elephants; we walked on the skin of bears who had been killed by this staunch hunter of living species. And it occurred to me that, God, I don't like being here. I don't want this, to be associated with death. And when we left, I said to my wife, 'I like the *people* — I truly do, they're gentle, they're kind, they're very gracious — but how can they live with all that death staring down at them?' And I went home and wrote 'Clean Kills and Other Trophies.'"

Fans of *Night Gallery* may notice that the scripted version of this story introduced a number of supernatural elements that gave the story a somewhat different trajectory. Serling had to make these changes to appease network executives who balked at the final scenes of his first version, the visceral impact of which pushed far beyond the staid boundaries of 1970s television decorum. The short story published here is his original, unadulterated vision.

Opening Narration

Our second painting this evening has to do with the stalker and the victim, the hunter and the hunted — that rare breed of Homo sapiens *whose love of butchery is not a sport but a consuming passion. Offered to you now, "Clean Kills and Other Trophies."*

They're Tearing Down Tim Riley's Bar

Rod Serling, while teaching a writing course at Ithaca College in 1972, remarked that "every writer has certain special loves, cer-tain special hang-ups, certain special preoccupations. In my case, it's a hunger to be young again, a desperate hunger to go back where it all began. And I think you'll see this as a running thread through a lot of things that I write."

The *Twilight Zone* dramas "Walking Distance" and "A Stop at Willoughby" explored with great sensitivity his hunger for respite and return. *Night Gallery*'s "They're Tearing Down Tim Riley's Bar," his gentle, lyrical study of human loss and expectation, is equally powerful and revealing. It would be the penultimate exercise on this theme in his career, followed only by his unproduced *Gallery* script, "The View of Whatever."

Contradictory accounts over how Serling intended to end this story still make the rounds as part of the behind-the-scenes lore of *Night Gallery*. Actor William Windom, who portrayed Randy Lane in "They're Tearing Down Tim Riley's Bar," claimed the first script he received had a downbeat ending, and that replacement pages arrived later that revised the tone from tragic to hopeful. Contradicting this account, Don Taylor, who cast Windom in the role and directed the episode for the series, had no such recollections. Any other accounts of what happened during production in the autumn of 1970 must yield to the weight of evidence Rod Serling left behind in his personal papers. All the completed drafts of this script have only one finale — the one he later translated into prose, the one you will read here. It can be considered his final thoughts on this very personal tale.

Opening Narration

Welcome, ladies and gentlemen, to an exhibit of the eerie and the oddball. Our first offering this evening: faces. Paint, pigment, and desperation — the quiet desperation of men over forty who keep hearing footsteps behind them and are torn between a fear and a compulsion to look over their shoulders. The painting is called "They're Tearing Down Tim Riley's Bar."

THE SOLE SURVIVOR

Ponderous yet stately; a giant floating city and yet with her vast decks converging into a single point at the bow, there was a suggestion of gracefulness and speed. Her four funnels spewed out trailing black columns of smoke against the cloudless sky. Far off in the distance little patches of fog blurred the horizon, but the visibility was almost unlimited.

The Lookout spotted the object first and called down to the bridge. "Object in the water," his metallic voice rasped through the speaker, "two miles ahead."

On the bridge the Officer of the Watch and the Quartermaster peered through their binoculars. A black dot bobbing in the gentle swell of the ocean, but clearly visible.

"Damned odd," the Officer of the Watch said, lowering his binoculars. "A lifeboat is what it is."

The Quartermaster kept the binoculars to his eyes. "Appears to be ... appears to be one survivor."

The Captain of the ship entered the bridge and moved to the ship's telephone on the wall, unhooking it and putting the mouthpiece close to his own mouth. "Lookout. Any signs of life?"

"I thought I saw a movement, sir," the Lookout's voice responded, "but I can't swear to it."

The Captain put the ship's telephone back on its hook and turned toward the two men flanking the wheel. "Starboard, five degrees," he said tersely to the Helmsman.

"Starboard, five degrees, sir."

The Captain turned to the Officer of the Watch. "Three long blasts, Mr. Wilson," he ordered.

The Officer of the Watch pulled a cord above him. There were three massive resounding blasts of noise. Then the Captain looked through his own binoculars. The black dot grew larger.

"Officer of the Watch," the Captain asked, "who's our best small-boats man?"

"That would be Mr. Richards, sir."

The Captain lowered his binoculars. "Ask him to come to the bridge."

"Mr. Richards to the bridge," the Officer of the Watch said into the ship's phone.

The Captain moved across the bridge to stand next to the Helmsman. Again he lifted the binoculars to his eyes. "I'll be damned," he said softly. "Looks to be a ... a woman." He chewed on the end of his moustache as the binoculars dropped; then he turned to the Officer of the Watch. "No reports of ships in distress in these waters?" It was a statement with just a shade of questioning inflection.

"No, sir."

"And yet," the Captain said musingly, "that's a ship's boat. There's no mistaking it."

A young Junior First Officer entered the bridge and saluted the Captain.

"Mr. Richards," the Captain said, "I want you to take starboard sea boat. I'm going to drop and recover you underway. Take a Signalman with you."

He turned to peer through the glass in front — the crow's-feet lines contracting with the habit of years. "We'll be making about five knots when we bring the boat abeam," he continued. "The lifeboat is about two miles away." He made rapid silent calculations inside his head. "This will give you seven minutes to waterline. I'll give two short blasts, which will be the executive for unhooking the forward falls and shearing off. I'll circle ship to port and pick you up in the same position. Understood?"

"Aye, aye, Captain," Mr. Richards said, with a salute.

"Then carry on." The Captain had already turned to the Quartermaster. "Stop engines," he continued.

"Stop engines," the Quartermaster repeated the order, but turned toward the Captain as he did so. Any slowing down, let alone going dead in the water, was a deadly serious business.

"You heard the order," the Captain said.

The Quartermaster nodded, then reached forward to turn an iron handle. "Stop engines," he repeated again.

"Starboard, two degrees," the Captain said to the Helmsman.

"Starboard, two degrees," the Helmsman repeated the order, turning the wheel slightly.

The Captain and the Officer of the Watch moved out to the open deck in front of the bridge. Again binoculars were raised. The black dot now looked about the size of a fist.

"Make out a name yet?" the Captain asked.

The Officer of the Watch shook his head. "Bit of a fog dead ahead, sir. And that lifeboat — or whatever she is — keeps moving in and out of her."

Again the Captain chewed on the corner of his moustache. "Bloody puzzlement," he murmured. "Ship's boat when there's no ship around. One survivor — and a woman at that. A bloody puzzlement." Then his voice took on the crisp tone of command. "Check seaboard," he continued.

The Officer of the Watch peered over the side railing. Halfway down the vast expanse of ship's side, a boat was being lowered. "Lowering away handsomely, sir."

The Captain stepped back inside the bridge. "What's our speed through water?" he asked the Quartermaster.

"Down to seven knots, sir."

The Captain turned to the Officer of the Watch, who'd followed him in. "And the range of the ship's boat?"

"Approximately a mile and a half now, sir," the Officer of the Watch answered.

"All engines slow astern," the Captain ordered.

"All engines slow astern."

"Check your sea boat again."

The Officer of the Watch went back outside and again looked over the railing. "At waterline, sir — after falls unhooked," he called out through the open door.

"Stand by," the Captain said. "Two short blasts."

The Quartermaster repeated the order.

"Speed?"

"Five knots, sir."

The Captain felt perspiration on his face. "Stop engines," he ordered.

"Stop engines," the Quartermaster repeated.

Again the voice of the Officer of the Watch came in from outside. "Ship's boat almost abeam," he announced.

The Captain wiped his face. "Two short blasts," he ordered.

"Two short blasts," came the Quartermaster's voice, and once again the pulsating crescendo of noise blasted through the stillness of the day.

"Sea boat's sheared off, sir," the Officer of the Watch informed him.

The Captain nodded. "Slow ahead, Quartermaster." Then he turned to the Helmsman. "Port, ten degrees."

"Aye, aye, sir," the Helmsman said, turning the wheel.

The Captain lifted up his binoculars, and already those gray little ghosts of doubt marched across his mind. The small and insignificant act of compassion, standing alone and embattled against the giant enemy that was war. Stop a ship that size on a clear and waveless day. God — the risk. The miserable risk. But there *were* laws of the sea that transcended the improvised callousness that passed for security in wartime — laws and customs that dated back to sails and oars; codes of human behavior that had to be honored.

The Captain shook his head as if clearing it of the extraneous little ghosts. "Have Signalman report condition of the survivor," he started to say, then broke off abruptly and frowned. "Mr. Wilson," he barked.

The Officer of the Watch reentered the bridge. "Sir?"

"On the bow of that ship's boat — do you make out something?"

The Officer of the Watch squinted through the binoculars. "Very faintly, sir," he said softly. "A name ...."

The binoculars fell. He stood there, mouth open. "That's quite impossible," he said to no one in particular. "Quite impossible."

"Impossible," the Captain said grimly, "or the product of someone's perverted sense of humor." He looked through his binoculars. "You'll be entering this in the log after the Dog Watch this evening, Mr. Wilson. I'll initial it." He lowered the binoculars. "Without my official corroboration, they'd have you up in front of a Board of Inquiry for drinking on duty."

He took a deep breath and moved toward the deck entrance. "I'll be on deck," he announced. "I want to be the first person to talk to that survivor — whoever she is."

He walked out on his little, muscle-knotted bandied sea legs, and his braided Captain's hat could be seen disappearing as he moved down the steps to the deck below.

"What did you see, sir?" the Quartermaster asked the Officer of the Watch.

He gestured toward his binoculars. "I can't make out anything now. She's turned in the swell, and her bow's to us."

"Well, I'll tell you, Q.M.," the Officer of the Watch said. "That is, I'll tell you what I think I saw — and what the Captain thinks *he* saw."

The other men on the bridge stared straight ahead, but there was a sudden and absolute silence.

"On the bow of that ship's boat," the Officer of the Watch said, "it appears to read ... it appears to read ... 'The Titanic'!"

They gently lifted the blanketed body of the woman over the railing onto A-deck and then placed it on a stretcher.

The small patches of fog had joined, and the sun was now blotted out. The scene looked funereal as passengers and crew surrounded the stretcher and stared down at it.

The Captain approached the group, and the sailors quickly moved aside as if in response to a silent command.

"Unconscious, sir," Richards said to the Captain.

The Captain leaned down, gently pulled aside the blanket to reveal the face of the unconscious body on the stretcher. The face was gray, pale, and bearded.

The Captain looked up towards Richards. "Unconscious ... and also a man."

"But dressed as a woman, sir —" Richards said.

The Captain straightened, pulled at his moustache, then gestured. "Take him to the Infirmary."

Several sailors lifted the stretcher and started to trudge down the deck. The Captain moved as if to follow them. Richards touched his arm.

"Captain?" Richards said. "They're pulling the lifeboat in on C-deck. I think you'd best look at it, sir. One blanket, that's all I found. No rescue packets, no life jackets, no flares —"

"Could have been lost at sea," the Captain said musingly. "Swept overboard —"

Richards shook his head. "That's not all that's odd, sir. Her condition —"

The Captain turned to him and frowned. "What about it?"

"She's so barnacled, sir — all crusted up to the waterline. It's as if she'd been afloat for —"

The Captain interrupted him. "For how long? Go ahead, say it: Since the *Titanic* hit an iceberg? And if that were the case, Mr. Richards — what do you suppose the condition of that man would be?"

Richards looked down the length of the deck as the stretcher disappeared inside. "He'd be a skeleton, sir," Richards said softly.

The Captain nodded. "That's a reasonable surmise," he said, his eyes squinting.

Richards couldn't read humor or sarcasm.

"So we come to the obvious conclusion, Mr. Richards," the Captain continued.

"Which is, sir?" Richards' voice was soft and somehow apologetic, as if the conclusions were obvious and were simply eluding him.

"Conclusions as follows, Mr. Richards," the Captain said, and this time there was just a shade of a smile underneath the moustache. "The man's been at sea for a week or two. Possibly three at the outside. But that's all."

"And the name on the ship's boat?" Richards asked.

"I'll tell you what, Mr. Richards," the Captain said. "When the gentleman regains consciousness, we'll ask him!"

The man lay in bed in the ship's Infirmary as night shrouded the ocean outside. There was no sound save for the vast humming turbines of the ship's engines; and then the quiet, hushed footsteps of the ship's doctor, who entered the room, went over to the bed, and stared down at the man. After a moment the Captain appeared at the open doorway. The doctor moved quickly over to him, pantomiming his wish that they converse elsewhere.

They moved into the doctor's office alongside the Infirmary room, and the doctor closed the door.

"Still unconscious?" the Captain asked.

The ship's doctor lit a pipe. "More like a … a coma."

"And his physical condition?"

The ship's doctor sucked in on his pipe, looked down at his desk, then up into the Captain's face. "Thin," he answered. "Obviously in shock. And his right foot —"

"What about it?" the Captain asked.

The ship's doctor looked grim and unhappy. "Frostbite," he answered.

The Captain studied the ship's doctor. "Frostbite? *In the month of May?* Let me ask you something, doctor — have you been on deck recently?"

The ship's doctor nodded. "Yes, sir, I have."

"Have you seen any icebergs?" the Captain asked.

The ship's doctor shook his head and smiled. "No, sir. Not a single iceberg."

The Captain leaned over the desk. Not a sarcastic man, he dredged up sarcasm to cover his own bewilderment. "You'd *know* an iceberg if you saw one?" he asked.

The ship's doctor stifled an explosive anger, but even at that his voice came out cold. "I'd also know a case of frostbite, Captain — even if I stumbled across it in equatorial Africa!"

There was the sound of a man's voice from the adjoining room — just the faintest of outcries. Both men tensed instantly; then the Captain followed the ship's doctor toward the connecting door and on into the Infirmary.

The man in the bed was sitting up, his eyes open and staring. Very slowly he turned to look at the two men who'd just entered the room.

"Feeling better?" the ship's doctor asked.

The man just stared at him, not responding.

"I think we'd best have a chat, you and I," the Captain said, with a brief look toward the ship's doctor, who nodded, turned, and left the room.

The Captain pulled up a chair alongside of the bed. He tried to keep his voice neutral. "Now, let's have it from the beginning," he said. "At approximately fourteen:thirty we found you in a ship's boat. On it was written 'The Titanic,' and in it — there was you and there was one blanket. Now, what I'd like to know is —"

The ship's bell rang nine times. Inside his office the ship's doctor checked desultorily the various patients' charts. His mind wasn't on it. At intervals he would lift up his head to listen to the muffled voices from the room alongside.

In that room the Captain had just left his chair. There was nothing neutral in his voice by that time. He felt nothing but frustration and helpless bewilderment. The survivor, after an hour and a half, still made no sense whatsoever.

"Surely you can't have been the sole survivor," the Captain said, obviously persisting along a familiar line. "After your boat was lowered, what about the crew, the other passengers?"

The survivor's eyes looked overly big, set deep in the emaciated face. "I ... I don't remember," he whispered. "All I remember is just drifting. Waking up in the boat ... and just drifting."

There was a tap on the door. The ship's doctor entered, looking at his watch.

The Captain made a gesture as if to say he was almost finished.

"And the name of your ship?" the Captain asked for perhaps the dozenth time.

"The *Titanic*," the survivor said.

The Captain pursed his lips, held his breath and then blew it out. "The *Titanic*, you say."

"Yes, sir. The *Titanic*."

The Captain looked toward the ship's doctor with a shrug, then over his shoulder toward the survivor. "And your name? Tell the ship's doctor your name."

The survivor looked around toward the ship's doctor. He closed his eyes tightly as if deep in thought.

The Captain's voice was much louder now. "The gentleman doesn't remember his name," he half-shouted. "The gentleman doesn't remember very damned much."

The ship's doctor made a little pantomiming gesture as if pleading for restraint.

The Captain shook his head and turned away, pacing restively.

"What do you recall?" the ship's doctor asked as he approached the bed, his voice soft.

The survivor opened his eyes. "We fouled an iceberg. It was a point on the starboard side. Then there was this ... shuddering noise — scraping — somewhere under the starboard bow." He shook his head. "That's all I remember," he added helplessly.

The ship's doctor turned from the patient toward the Captain, who had halted his pacing.

The Captain looked disgusted. He retraced his steps over to the bed, this time scaling down his voice, though the impatience and distaste showed through. "You were dressed in women's clothing," he said. "Can you explain that?"

Silence.

"Can you?"

Still silence.

"You have no idea?" The Captain's voice was now that of a British officer in a Court of Inquiry. It just happened to take place in the ship's Infirmary. "Perhaps," he said, after a pause, "perhaps you won't mind if I take a stab at an explanation."

The man on the bed kept his eyes averted.

"Perhaps you put that dress on," the Captain said, "to gain access to a lifeboat. Could that be it?"

The survivor whispered. "I don't know."

The Captain moved closer to the bed. "You don't know? Is that what you said? I think you do."

The survivor's face seemed to shrivel, and he cringed, as though half-expecting a physical blow.

The ship's doctor put a restraining hand on the Captain's arm and again warned him with a look.

The Captain nodded, jammed his hands into his pockets, looked up toward the ceiling, then back down to the survivor on the bed. "We'll talk again later," he said. "Perhaps when you've rested, some of the answers that presently prove so elusive will manage to wriggle their way to the surface."

He turned on his heel and walked out of the room.

The ship's doctor looked from one to the other and was about to follow the Captain when the survivor painfully inched his way back to a partial sitting position. "Doctor," he called out hoarsely.

The ship's doctor turned to him.

"What year is it?"

The ship's doctor frowned. "What year do you think it is?"

The survivor lowered his head back down on the pillow. "It's 1912. Isn't it? Isn't it 1912?"

The ship's doctor's voice was very soft. "Try to get some more sleep," he said. "There'll be someone in attendance at all times."

He moved out into the passageway, closing the door behind him. The Captain was standing there. The ship's doctor tried to smile. "I should very much like to know what this is all about, Captain."

The Captain looked toward the closed door. "And so should I. Obviously it's some kind of hoax. And obviously it's an outrageous one. And there's no doubt in my mind that he's been carefully coached."

"Coached?" the ship's doctor asked.

The Captain nodded. "And in spite of that — he supplied us a few pieces to the puzzle."

The ship's doctor looked bewildered. "Like what?" he asked.

" 'Fouled the iceberg,' That's what he said." The Captain pointed to the closed door. " 'Iceberg, a point on the starboard bow.' Doctor, that's a sailor talking. *But in whose service?*"

Slowly, his shoulders hunched, the Captain started toward the stairway. The ship's doctor followed him. At the foot of the stairs the Captain stopped and looked straight ahead, deep in thought.

The ship's doctor's voice was tentative. "I don't think I understand," he began.

The Captain turned to him, his voice grim. "I'm wondering if it's possible your patient was put adrift for a very specific purpose."

"Purpose? You've lost me, Captain."

The Captain put one foot on the first rung of stairs. "To slow us down, man. To make us alter course. I know that sounds altogether incredible, doctor … but you know, there *is* a war on."

He looked down the length of the passageway toward the Infirmary door, then turned and started a slow walk up the stairs, leaving the ship's doctor staring up at him.

On the bulkhead wall a life preserver made a small sideward movement in a sudden swell. On it was stencilled, "The Lusitania."

An infirmary attendant came out of the patient's room into the passageway just as the ship's doctor came down the stairs. The ship's bell rang eleven times. The attendant balanced a tray with two plates of untouched food. The ship's doctor noted it briefly. "Not eating?" he asked.

The attendant shook his head. "Not a morsel, sir — which is odd, if you'll forgive me. Poor bloke's thin as a drainpipe. Hasn't got a pound of flesh on his bones. Looks to be proper starving is what he looks." He looked down at the tray. "Still — I couldn't get a cracker into him."

The ship's doctor moved past him to the Infirmary door, opened it, and entered. A small orange night light sent darting shadows around the room. The ship's doctor approached the bed and leaned over.

The survivor was awake, his eyes wide open.

"No appetite, I'm told," the ship's doctor said.

The survivor stared straight up at the ceiling. "What time is it?"

"Shortly after eight."

The survivor's voice sounded hollow, strangely like some kind of sepulchral confession. "Dog Watch just ended," he said.

Again the ship's doctor tried to read something in the skin-tight, unrevealing face. Despite himself, he felt an unbidden thrill. What if the man were a spy? What if he knew something that no one else knew? What if he asked the time because he knew that at a certain hour —

The ship's doctor unconsciously shook his head. Paranoia, he thought. But God, in a ship at sea during wartime, you could conjure up any kind of jeopardy. He forced an evenness to his tone. "Were you a member of the *Titanic's* crew?" he asked.

"Stoker."

The ship's doctor smiled, or at least tried to smile. "Well," he said in a bedside tone, "if you want to ship out again when we reach London, I'd recommend taking some nourishment."

The man on the bed turned to study him. The oversized eyes in the undersized face seemed to glow fanatically in the night light. "This ship's the *Lusitania*," he said softly, as if trying to authenticate that which he already knew.

"That's right," the ship's doctor answered.

The survivor lifted a thin, veined hand to his beard-stubbled chin. "It's 1915," he said.

The ship's doctor nodded.

"I've been in that lifeboat for three years."

It was chilling just to hear him say it — chilling. To voice the impossible as if it were a matter of record.

"Well, now," the ship's doctor said, his voice nervous. "Well, now — we both know you couldn't have been in a lifeboat for three years."

The room, the ship's doctor noted, in another portion of his mind, had grown suddenly silent. It was as if the engines had stopped — that constant, rhythmic, pounding noise of dynamos that somehow fused into the subconscious and disappeared — now it was as if they were nonexistent. The room was utterly silent.

The survivor's voice seemed louder in the stillness. "A question to you, doctor," he said. "How do you know what I've told you isn't possible? Listen to me — listen to me and then tell me if you still think it's impossible."

Not a spy, the ship's doctor thought. Spies fitted molds. Cold, callous, always planning kind of chaps. But this man ... those haunted eyes ... the anguish that seemed so much a part of him — deranged, of course, but not a spy.

He leaned forward. "Tell me about it," he said.

For a moment the survivor's lips moved with no words forthcoming; then he abruptly tore his gaze from the ship's doctor and stared fixedly toward the wall. His voice sounded choked. "Have you ever been frightened, doctor? I mean, so frightened you'd do anything to survive? Have you?"

Humor him, the ship's doctor thought. Always humor the deranged. Give them at least that much comfort.

"Fortunately," the ship's doctor said, "I've never found myself in that kind of situation."

The skeletal face turned to him again. "I have," the survivor said. He took a deep breath. "She was down by the bow and going fast. When I tried to get into a lifeboat, they stopped me. No crew members. Just women and children."

"That's a traditional rule of the sea," the ship's doctor said, his voice slightly aimless, like a kind of absentminded teacher.

The survivor stared at him. "Sure. Sure — unless you're standing on a tilted deck heading into icy water that'll kill you in three minutes. Then you don't think about traditional rules of the sea."

A silence. The ship's doctor waited. "So you put on a dress," he said finally.

The survivor nodded. "And a muffler to hide my face. And I knocked a half a dozen people aside and got on. While they were lowering her, one of the cables broke. She capsized. But I hung on. Somehow I hung on. When she hit the water, I was the only one who had."

The silence, the ship's doctor thought — the incredible silence of the room and the ship. No ship's engines. No creaking bulkheads. No metallic tinkle of dishes or glassware. No squeak of a ship's lamp as it undulated slowly in the ocean's swell. There was absolutely no sound.

And then the survivor's voice continued. "The ship's band was playing. Some kind of hymn. And there was this … this great wailing cry. I could look up at the deck and see faces along the rail. Hundreds of faces. Then there was this explosion. She was going down by the bow, and everything inside that ship was moving. Pianos, furniture, deck chairs — everything … all crashing down into the bow. And then there was this … this *cry*. Then one by one the funnels disappeared … and then the ship. Then there was nothing but bodies floating. Stars … dead calm … and bodies."

The ship's doctor felt mesmerized.

The voice of the survivor continued in a dead monotone. The night light swayed back and forth from the ceiling.

"An illusion," the ship's doctor finally managed to say. "Understand? It *had* to be an illusion. You *couldn't* have been on the *Titanic*. You couldn't have survived in an open boat for three years."

He rose from the chair, bewildered and shaken by the spectral voice and the skeletal figure who spoke so calmly and so believingly about something that was beyond belief.

"There is an explanation for this," he said. "A rational, believable, altogether understandable explanation. And it'll come out eventually. In the meantime —

The survivor interrupted him. "In the meantime, doctor — let me tell you something."

The ship's doctor felt his hand shake, and it was suddenly hard to breathe.

The man on the bed swung his legs over the side and rested them on the floor. Skin and bones. Skeleton. Just a frame covered by a thin parchment of flesh.

"You're going to be hit by a torpedo," the man said, "off the Old Head of Kindale. You're going down in eighteen minutes flat."

The voice was so soft, so matter-of-fact, that for a moment the ship's doctor found it difficult to connect tone with words. What had the man said? Something about a torpedo? Something about going down in eighteen minutes? And what had the Captain said? The man was a spy.

"By God," the ship's doctor said finally. "By God, you *are* a German agent."

For the first time the survivor smiled — thin, slit mouth just slightly turned up. "A German agent? I wish ... I wish to God I was." He shook his head. "No, doctor, I'm no agent. Not a spy. Not a saboteur. But you know something? I'm beginning to understand just what I *am*."

Again the blanketing silence.

"What ... are ... you?" the ship's doctor asked.

The survivor stood up, swaying slightly, holding onto the night table for support. "I'll tell you what I am, doctor," he said. "I'm a Flying Dutchman, built of flesh, blood, and bones. Damned and doomed. An eternity of lifeboats ... rescues ... and then —"

"— And then forever being picked up by doomed ships," the ship's doctor said to the Captain as they sat in his cabin. An early-morning light filtered through the porthole as the night gave way to day.

The Captain sat behind his desk and folded his hands behind his head. "Justice, of the poetic sort," he said, smiling.

"He believes it," the ship's doctor said.

The Captain's smile was fixed. "Does he, now? He believes it." He leaned farther back in his chair. "Very fanciful," he said. "Altogether bizarre." Then he put his hands down on top of the desk. "Except for a very notable flaw. If this is *his* damnation, *his* punishment for an act of cowardice —"

"He believes that it is," the ship's doctor interrupted.

The Captain shook his head. "So we take a torpedo and share his punishment?" He smiled. "Not exactly fair, you'll admit, since none of us have done anything to make us damned and doomed, eh?"

"It doesn't work that way," the ship's doctor said, as if pleading a case. "He tells me that when the torpedo hits — only *he'll* be aware of it. We're only here to ... to people the scene, so to speak."

The Captain rose from behind the desk, the smile gradually fading. "So. And following that logic, it means that you and I are —"

"Phantoms," the ship's doctor said. "Phantoms, Captain. Ghosts of what we were."

The Captain walked over to the porthole and stared out at the brightening sky. "Now, that's interesting," he said. "Especially interesting in light of the fact that I don't feel at all like a phantom. To the contrary, doctor, I feel —"

He turned as he spoke, and whatever words were to follow were choked off and left deep inside his throat.

He was alone in the room. There was no ship's doctor. Inside his mind the machinery of logic roared and pulsated; the mental process that manufactured rationale, that explained away the impossible, that offered up the clues, the excuses, the reasons to explain the totally unexplainable.

The room was empty.

The ship's doctor had disappeared.

And the machinery in the Captain's head stripped gears and went off in screaming tangents, thoughts colliding with thoughts and terror laying claim to the debris. Like some kind of partially destroyed robot, he forced his legs over to the ship's phone on the wall and tried to reach the bridge.

"Bridge, this is the Captain. Come in, bridge. This is the Captain, bridge. Come in —"

Three decks above him the bridge was empty of men. The dials of the instruments moved; the ship's phone undulated gently on its hook; the needle of the giant compass above the Helmsman's wheel moved left and right in sporadic little stops and gos.

And then the Captain's cabin was empty.

The survivor forced himself through empty passageways, down silent decks, into cavernous salons and mausoleum-like dining rooms. When he reached the deck, he went directly to the rail and looked out at the quiet sea. And then he saw it. A tiny black broom handle sticking up above the water.

"Periscope," he screamed. "Periscope off the starboard bow!"

He looked wildly up and down the empty deck. "Periscope," he screamed again, "off the starboard bow!"

He raced up a ladderway to the deck above him. And then he saw the torpedo. It slivered through the water at a breathless speed, leaving a wake of frosty bubbles. Then another torpedo, and still a third. His world exploded into a flash of blinding whiteness. He felt an incredible pain, and then for a time he felt nothing at all.

The ocean liner, gleaming white and graceful as a porpoise, sped swiftly across the quiet sea.

On the bridge came the voice of a Lookout through the ship's speaker. "Object dead ahead," the metallic voice rasped.

The men on the bridge lifted up binoculars and peered through the glass.

"Incredible," said the Officer of the Watch.

"What is it?" asked the Quartermaster.

"A ship's boat," the Officer of the Watch answered. "Appears to be ... one survivor."

A tall, gray-bearded Captain entered the bridge. "Any sign of life?" he asked.

"One survivor, sir," the Officer of the Watch responded, "but —"

"But what?"

The Officer of the Watch took off his binoculars and handed them to the Captain. "You'd best look for yourself, sir."

The Captain lifted the binoculars and peered through the glass. "That can't be," he said in a quiet little voice. He lowered the binoculars, then turned toward the Officer of the Watch. "Get a small boatman and lower him immediately. We'll stop for a recovery." Again he raised the binoculars. "I think someone must be playing a joke. You read the name of the bow, Carlos?"

The Officer of the Watch gulped. "Yes, sir, I do. It reads ... 'The Lusitania,' sir."

The Captain took a deep breath. "The *Lusitania*," he said. "Sunk — forty-odd years ago. And this is one of her lifeboats?" He shook his head, rejecting the entire thing. "Stop engines," he ordered.

"Stop engines," the Quartermaster repeated.

"Starboard, two degrees," the Captain said to the Helmsman.

The Helmsman, following his compass, turned the wheel slightly to the right and felt a combination chill and sweat. He had to wipe the perspiration from his brow where little rivulets of water were dripping down from his seaman's cap — a cap which read "S.S. Andrea Doria."

There was a ship's whistle, and then the grinding halt of the engines; and in the little lifeboat the survivor looked toward the approaching rescuers. He wondered how long it would be this time. And how would the death come. Then he felt the jar and scrape of the other boat hitting the gunwales of his own. He fainted as eager arms reached out to pull him to what they thought was safety.

MAKE ME LAUGH

His mother was a cooch dancer, his father a carnival donicker, and he arrived on earth a squalling, protesting lard-ass — fat and ugly, screaming around the clock, as if someone had already told his fortune and whispered it into his mother's womb for him to hear.

His last name was Slatsky — and they named him Jacob. But no one ever called him by name, even as an infant. They called him "Fats" — always as a description and never as an endearment.

By the time he was five, his infant ugliness had taken root in his piggish little face and obese little body. When he was ten, his father abandoned his mother. When he was fifteen, his mother deserted him. And by the time he was twenty, he had forsaken his name and become Jackie Slater.

Jackie Slater. A balding, baggy-pants fat man who did stand-up monologues in third-rate "nightclubs" — smelly little places with broken neon signs — and he would stand in front of a cheap and distorting microphone, wheezing out broad burlesque in between arthritic acrobats and over-the-hill, big-thighed dancing girls, playing to bored boozers who had either heard his jokes or didn't want to hear them.

Jackie Slater. An overweight thief of other people's material, trying to be Jackie Gleason, Sam Levenson, or Joe Miller; trying to be anybody and everybody just to squeeze out laughter from the grim dark silhouettes sitting at tables beyond the spotlight. He was bad. A coaxer and a cajoler. A classless clown, freakish but not funny. Gross. Wheedling. Desperately cute. A hippopotamus in ruffled panties, waddling around the stage, sweating his life away in one-nighters.

Myron's Mecca was a roadhouse outside of Corning, New York. On the walls were faded murals from the Arabian Nights, looking like bad cartoons. The two waitresses, dressed as harem girls, looked like two crone rejects from a long-dead Sultan; the bartender wore a Shriner's fez with a bare spot underneath a beaded scimitar with the faded lettering "Scranton, Pa." The place smelled of stale beer mixed occasionally with the wafting salty scent of a fresher liquid when the door leading to the rest rooms was opened and closed. Beaded curtains had been hung behind a six-foot-square platform which served as a stage, and there was a dissonant four-piece combo, now mercifully silent as Jackie Slater stood on the stage, clutching a microphone and dying.

"You like this suit? It's a chopped-liver gray. Nice fit? My girl friend says it looks more like a convulsion."

Silence in the audience. A half-dozen bored drunks. One short, staccato burst of laughter, and then a high-pitched female giggle. On Jackie's pale, perspiring, uncooked dough face, a hopeful halfsmile, quickly erased. The man had poured a drink down the dress of a peroxide bimbo and laughed. The bimbo had giggled.

"Yessir — more like a convulsion," Jackie perspired and repeated and milked.

"It is — you ain't," said a man at the bar, and the bartender chuckled.

Jackie gripped the microphone tighter. "Just the other day," he said, "I met some very good friends of mine out in front of the Plaza in New York. That's where I was living at the time. Out in front of the Plaza."

Silence from the audience, then somebody coughed. Somebody else overturned a glass.

"Yessir," Jackie repeated, "that's where I was living at the time — out in front of the Plaza."

"We heard you the first time, fat man," yelled the man at the bar. Then he turned to the bartender. "When do the dames dance?"

The bartender scratched his forehead underneath the fez. "Anytime now."

The heckler looked toward Jackie. "What does it take to get him off? A lynching?"

The bartender grinned. "He's great for all the other acts. He makes 'em look so good."

"I believe it," said the man. He cupped his hands in front of his mouth and yelled toward Jackie. "Hey, klutz — you can get off now. The trained seal just recuperated."

Jackie smiled a sick smile and waved. There was always one; always one smart ass in the audience. Usually drunk. Usually big. Always belligerent. Jackie looked around the room. His smile was a suspended, crooked thing — like a billboard that had slipped. And he waddled around, back and forth, holding on to the microphone, slipping the back of his hands together, grunting like a seal. Oh, God, why didn't they laugh? And even as he probed for the next gag, the cheapness of the place rose up in front of his eyes in waves. It was as if his entire world was Myron's Mecca, and the giggling broad, the two loaded Teamsters, the bored bartender, and the former Pacific Fleet champion sitting at the bar were his own private ghosts, hired to haunt him through eternity. They were always the same. And his performance was always the same. Tonight was like all the others. A long line of funerals. He did a little half-step, yanked up on the microphone cord, pointed a finger at the half-sleeping combo, then turned to face the eight people in the room. "And now," he shrieked, "ladies and gentlemen — four of the most beautiful, talented ladies you've ever met in your life —"

"Jesus, it's about time," yelled the man at the bar.

"Here they are," said Jackie, ignoring him. "The Finger Lakes Fandangos."

The combo, chords apart, spewed out a ragged fanfare.

Jackie bowed low at imaginary applause, took another little dancing half-step, deposited the microphone in its stand, and walked off the stage and through a side door that led to the rest rooms and his own dressing room. The Finger Lakes Fandangos passed him en route — eight sagging tits in sequins.

The voice of the man at the bar drowned out the combo. "Oh, Jesus. Out goes the hippo — in come the dogs!"

Jackie walked down the dark, narrow corridor to the tiny little cubicle set between "Men" and "Women." He opened the door and went inside. From either side came the sound of flushing through the thin walls, mixed with the snores of his agent, Jules Kettleman, who lay asleep on the threadbare sofa.

Jules was a gaunt, bony little man with a perpetually startled look in his eyes. He awoke with a start and sat up. "How'd it go?" he asked.

Jackie sat down heavily in front of a cracked mirror on a rickety card chair — the only other furniture in the room. He averted his reflection in the mirror and forced a smile. "For a first shot ... for a first shot, maybe not so bad. I'm gonna rework it a little bit before the next show."

He rose and banged his head on the yellow bulb that hung by a naked wire. It swung back and forth, sending out little shadows of light and dark that played hide-and-seek with the jowled flesh of his face. He was conscious of Jules staring at him, and there was a long and deadly silence.

"Goddamn it — *say it.*"

"Say wot? Whaddya wanna hear, Jackie?"

Jackie turned to him. "It would've been nice to hear you push a coupla laughs out there. Or maybe bang your hands together a few times. Honest to God, Jules — I'm playin' in front of Forest Lawn

— and you're in here like it was a federal law to be horizontal after the sun goes down."

He turned back toward his reflection, his bald dome, with the eight or ten straggling hair strands, glistening in the yellow light — like an ivory ruin with weeds coming up through the cracks.

"Didn't go over so well, huh?" Jules's voice was soft and knowing.

"That's the only tomb with a stage in it," Jackie said as he sat back down in the chair.

"That's the only stage with a corpse on it," a new voice said.

Jackie turned in the squeaking chair to look toward the open door.

Myron Mishkin stood there. He was the owner. He entered the room — a dyspeptic-looking tall man in a funeral-parlor-blue suit who took the step into the room like a man walking into a sewer, afraid to touch anything.

Jules started to sweat. "He warms up slow, Mr. Mishkin."

"It's a hundred and two out there," Mishkin said. "This guy couldn't warm up in a boiler room."

Jackie tried to laugh. It turned his voice ragged. "That's a tough audience, Mr. Mishkin. You'll give me that, won't you?"

"I'll tell ya what I'll give ya," Mishkin said through a barely lit cigar in his teeth. "Papers to walk. Do the last show, then cut."

"You said three weekends —" Jules began, slightly whining.

Mishkin turned to him. "That was before I heard him. You *are* his agent — isn't that the idea?"

"Twenty-four years, Mr. Mishkin." Jules tried to say it proudly.

Mishkin put his hand on the doorknob. "Then book the schmuck in the Air Force Museum." He pointed his cigar at Jackie. "This guy don't tell jokes — he goes on bombing missions. Do the last show, and I'll tell the bartender to pay ya off."

He started out the door. Jackie got to his feet and followed him out.

"Wait a minute, Mr. Mishkin. Please. You can't ace me out after one lousy show." He started toward Jules as if for confirmation.

Mishkin took the cigar out of his teeth. "I can't?" he asked. He looked toward Jules and jerked a thumb at Jackie. "Read him the contract."

Jackie felt the age-old panic. The fantasy again — the nightmare. The whole world was Myron's Mecca. And Myron Mishkin was the Great Omniscient Ass Kicker in charge of the universe. He presided at Jackie's nightly funerals, Jackie's failures, the busts, the flops, the crap-outs — the daily, weekly, monthly boots out of the door.

"Mr. Mishkin ... look, Mr. Mishkin ... it's a tough house. Honest to God. It's a tough house. But if I could have a coupla weeks —"

Mishkin looked at Jackie's hand on his arm and very gingerly removed it.

"Mr. Mishkin." Jackie's voice trembled. "An act's gotta build. I mean — you gotta allow a coupla weeks for word of mouth."

"I do?" Mishkin stared at him. "Honest to God — I gotta allow a coupla weeks for word of mouth?"

Jackie took hope. He whirled around toward Jules. "Tell him, Julie. Will ya tell him? Tell him about that gig in Buffalo. Six weeks held over. And capacity, man. In a tough room — lemme tell ya. But when I get started, man, I zoom. I could fill the Hollywood Bowl." He laughed, shrill and high-pitched. "Tell him, Julie. Go ahead, tell him."

Mishkin looked from one to the other. "Unasked," he said softly, putting the cigar back into his mouth. "Unasked, I give ya the following opinion." He took out the cigar and pointed it again at Jackie. "You couldn't fill a men's room with free shoeshines. I'm strictly truck trade here, but they know what they like. And you, they don't like. A piece of advice, Mr. Slater — from an old-time saloon keeper. This is your agent here? Well, you tell him to buy you a correspondence course in diesel-engine fixing. Or maybe the Regular Army. But he should get rid of ya."

His cigar went out, and he extracted a kitchen match from a side pocket, then scratched it against the shiny surface of the seat of his pants and lit the cigar. "Slater — as God is my witness — you don't have enough talent to pay ten percent to yourself — let alone that poor putz over there who books you."

Mishkin turned and walked down the corridor, passing the Finger Lakes Fandangos as they came out from the stage — a quartet of rouged and powdered beef.

Jackie moved back into the room, past Jules, and slumped down into the chair. He closed his eyes for a moment, then opened them and looked at his reflection. "You wanna hear somethin', Julie?" he said, whispering. "I was a fat, ugly little kid the day I was born. I had eight sets of foster parents before I was seventeen. They used to play jokes on me. Like when I'd come home from school — they'd moved."

Jules tried to chuckle, but it caught in his throat. He just looked down at the floor.

"One of them," Jackie said, quietly, "sent me to a Y.M.C.A. camp one summer. Y'know what the kids used to do there for kicks? They pushed me off the dock. Like every day, they pushed me off the dock. And then they'd all laugh. So I figured ... I figured that's what I'd do with my life. I'd make people laugh."

Jules kept his eyes fixed on the floor, but he made a little gesture, spreading out his hands at his sides. "You made some people laugh, Jackie."

Jackie closed his eyes. "Once," he said, "once I really got a boff from a guy in a men's room. I had this toup — this hairpiece. Black curly hair. And I'd left my date in the restaurant. Beautiful chick. And I went to the toilet ... and when I was finished ... I bent over to flush the john — and the toup fell in the toilet. You shoulda heard that guy. Like he started to cry, he laughed so hard."

Jackie turned to stare at Jules. "That's the story of my life, Julie. I keep fallin' in toilets." Then he turned back to stare at himself in the mirror. "I'm a second-rate schlep, goin' nowhere. And after twenty-four years of scratching each other's backs — we're still doin' one-nighters in garbage dumps. Julie — how right am I?"

Jules shrugged and said nothing.

"Well, I'll tell ya somethin'," Jackie continued. "I wish ... I wish I could make everybody laugh. That's what I wish. I'd give up everything I got. One trunk with the locks busted. Two suits and a sport coat. The wardrobe. Complete. One knitted tie with a hole in it and one that spells out, 'Will you kiss me in the dark, baby?' when the lights are out. One pair of shoes with lifts — one pair of sneakers."

Jules sniffled.

"Everything I got," Jackie said. "Everything. Just to make people laugh."

Then very slowly he put his face in his hands and he began to cry.

Jules swallowed, sniffled again, pulled out his handkerchief, and looked at this weeping whale in the chair. He wanted to reach out and touch him, say something gentle ... something kind. But in the back of his fifty-seven-year-old agent's mind, the thought came to him. Oh, God, but Jackie was right. He could break his balls for the next twenty years, lining up the one-nighters, counting out his ten-percent in nickels and dimes, and telling this poor, no-talent hippo that he was the greatest — when they both knew you could blow only so much smoke up anyone's butt until you had to acknowledge defeat and officially surrender. He thought all this as he tiptoed quietly out of the room. Jackie was the last of the stable. Most of them gone. Some of them dead and buried. All of them either has-beens or never-wases. And as he walked down the corridor, he thought some more. Maybe he could find some stacked broad who'd sing topless. Or maybe he could latch onto a magician who did dirty tricks. He'd have to find some kind of act. He'd just have to scrounge. And scrounging, Jules Kettleman had done all his life. It wasn't his fault, he thought, as he went out a side door into the alley, that he always unearthed dogs. Dogs, hambones, and fat Pagliaccis who planted their big asses on a wailing wall and wondered why they got carbuncles instead of laughs.

"It's to weep," he said to himself as he walked out the alley toward the street. "Not to laugh — but to weep."

Inside the dressing room, Jackie Slater had stopped his crying and was practicing his routines in front of the mirror. "... and this one fag said, 'I didn't know we had a Navy —' "

Jackie Slater got drunk and forgot that Jules Kettleman wasn't in his dressing room when he'd finished the last show. And now he was drunker and didn't even remember who Jules Kettleman was. It was 2:30 in the morning, and he was the next-to-last customer in the Mark Twain Bar, a block from his motel. He sat with mammoth buttocks overlapping the bar stool, fondling his seventh bourbon.

The bartender was eating a sandwich in one of the empty booths, then rose and came around the other side of the bar and looked at Jackie. "Your name Slater?" he asked.

Jackie nodded.

The bartender reached into his apron pocket for a folded piece of paper. He tossed it on the bar. "Some guy came in earlier. He left this for you."

Jackie blinked at it. "What is it?" he asked.

The bartender shrugged. "A note, I guess — for you. Some guy named ... Kettleman."

Jackie reached for the paper, unfolded it, and started to read it upside down. He blinked, then threw the paper back. "Would *you* read it for me?"

"You mean out loud?" the bartender asked.

"Right out loud."

The bartender beamed as he unfolded the paper. Pouring drinks in that kind of flea-bag saloon was a listening job. Forever listening. And usually it was the tortured tomes of misunderstood husbands, depression-ridden salesmen on the way down, or the blurred wisdom of all drunks who turn philosopher whenever they get bagged. He cleared his throat like a TV announcer and read aloud. " 'Dear Jackie. Please don't hate me for taking a run-out. But I'm as desperate as you are, and I've got to have bread. There's a steel-guitar band in Philadelphia —' "

Jackie upset his glass on the bar, then reached over and yanked the paper from the bartender's hand. He looked at it briefly through swimming eyeballs, then crumpled it up and threw it on the floor.

"Son of a bitch," said Jackie. Then he pointed at his empty glass.

The bartender shrugged and poured a shot into it. "What do you do?" he asked.

"What do I do? I'm a comic."

The bartender surveyed him dourly. "A comic?"

Jackie nodded vigorously. "And Kettleman is my agent. Was my agent. I hope his frigging steel guitar band rusts!"

"Where you been playin'?" the bartender asked.

"At Myron's Mecca," Jackie responded. "I did two shows. Just two shows." He downed his drink. "And I will never again set foot in Myron's Mecca."

The bartender started to wipe the bar, looking up at the clock over his shoulder. "I gather you didn't kill 'em in Myron's Mecca."

Jackie drained the glass. "How could I? They were already deceased." He tapped at the glass with a forefinger.

"I'm closin'," said the bartender.

"One more."

The bartender shrugged and poured out another shot.

Jackie held up his glass. "I give you Corning, New York," he toasted. "I give you Myron's Mecca. Six tables with a pallbearer at each one of them."

He finished the drink, put the glass down, and lumbered to his feet. It was at this point that he took note of the other customer in the bar.

Sitting cross-legged on a bar stool, dressed in a cape, upturned tasseled bedroom slippers, and a turban housing a cracked ruby, was a tiny little man with an iodine-colored face who looked like Sam Jaffe playing Gunga Din. He was looking out the corner of his eye toward Jackie, then turned on the bar stool to face him, unfolding his tiny little pipestem legs as he did so.

"We have not met, yefendi," he said in a fluty little voice. "Chatterje is the name. Miracles by profession."

Jackie blinked at him through blurred, bloodshot eyes. "Miracles?"

Chatterje smiled a tiny apologetic little smile. "Miracles."

"That's what I need," Jackie said, "a miracle. Not a big son of a bitch of a miracle — but a lousy little miracle. You know what, Mr. Chatterje? You are face to face with Mr. Unlucky."

Chatterje got off the stool and walked over to Jackie. "Forgiveness, Mr. Slater — but compared to me, you are the winner of the Irish Sweepstakes. You are the owner of the 1969 New York Mets. And on the day they repealed Prohibition — you are the Little Old Wine Maker."

Jackie looked down at the dark face and the black, slightly clouded, shoebutton eyes. He patted the little man's shoulder. "Mr. Chatterje — you don't know what trouble is. You know that? You are now looking at a shipmaker in the desert, a jewel cutter with the palsy, and an opera singer with laryngitis."

Chatterje held up his hands as if in protest and shook his head back and forth. "Reflect, if you will, Mr. Slater, this undersized guru who stands in front of you — this child of adversity —"

"Mr. Chatterje," Jackie interjected, "I played a B'nai B'rith convention in New Rochelle where they wanted to replace me with an Arab —"

The bartender looked from one to the other, like watching a Ping-Pong match, then started to untie his apron. "Maybe fifty thousand people are in this town," he said to his reflection in the mirror, "and who do I get? The Formaldehyde Twins. I gotta open up the only morgue with a liquor license in the whole state of New York." He turned from the mirror. "Why the hell don't you two guys go out and get mugged someplace?"

Chatterje folded his hands together. "Preferable," he said morosely. "Decidedly preferable to what is in store for me. Death — certainly before dishonor." He looked up at Jackie. "You, Mr. Slater, are yet a young man with much ahead of you. It need not always be Myron's Mecca. You could yet make it on the *Ed Sullivan Show*. I, on the other hand, am fingering the tassels at the far end of my rope. Let the Pale Horseman gallop in now. Let a celestial tailor enter to measure me for a shroud. For by dawn tomorrow, if I do not perform a miracle — I am relieved of my powers and I have dishonored my ancestors for centuries back."

The bartender went to the front door and lowered a shade. "So work a miracle already," he said, "but do it outside."

The turbaned little man shrugged. "There is no willing recipient," he said. "There is no soul trusting enough to allow this poor guru to conjure up a blessing." He fingered the cracked ruby of his turban. "I am without hope," he said. "I am a dispossessed soul, tiptoeing in agony across the wasteland of my shattered dreams."

"So tiptoe the hell outta here, Swami," the bartender said, preparing the night lock on the door.

Chatterje turned on his Arabian slippers and started toward the door.

Jackie reached out and grabbed his arm. "Wait a minute," he said. He studied Chatterje's face. "What is it with the miracle?"

Chatterje smiled sadly. "You are now diddling with the essence! That is what it is all about. Miracles. Every miracle-making guru

must work a wonder at least once a month. I am in arrears. Hence
— disaster."

Jackie focused his swimming eyeballs. "What kinda miracle?"
he asked.

Chatterje shrugged again. "Name it."

"I got a choice?" Jackie asked.

"You should only ask."

"Could you ... could you get me on the *Ed Sullivan Show?*"

"Most likely."

"Could you get me four weeks at the Sands in Vegas?"

"With options."

A dream started to build. Jackie clutched the little man's silk
vest and almost lifted him off the floor. "Could you ... could you
—"

"Speak, yefendi," Chatterje said.

"Could you fix it?" Jackie whispered. "Could you fix it so that I
could make people laugh?"

He held his breath, waiting for the dream to burst apart.

"Make people laugh?" Chatterje repeated. "Hysterically,
yefendi. Uncontrollably. Laughter beyond your wildest dreams."

Jackie's mouth was wide open. "Do it," he whispered again.

"Do it?" Chatterje repeated softly.

"Make a miracle," Jackie said, his voice shaking.

Chatterje gnawed on his lower lip. "This moment?"

"You gotta make a miracle by morning," Jackie said. "So make
a miracle on me. Fix it so's I can make people laugh!"

Chatterje put a forefinger to his mouth. "It shall be done ...
but —"

"But," Jackie shouted out loud, "there's a 'but,' huh? But what?
What comes now? The payoff, huh? The small print? The strings?"

Chatterje winced. "Yefendi," he said, "please —" He held up
his hands again. "Candor dictates certain prior admissions. Before a
miracle is wrought — it is necessary that I leave no truth unspoken.

This is a cardinal rule amongst the Order of Working Miracle Gurus." He took a deep breath. "In the hierarchy of my art ... how shall I say ... I am something less than proficient. That is to say — I am given to small imperfections in the miracles wrought."

Jackie blinked at him. The dream still hovered but was beginning to fade. "What kind of imperfections?" he asked breathlessly.

"Insignificant," Chatterje said with a shrug. He held up forefinger to thumb. "Small. Itsy-bitsy. But — it is necessary that I acquaint you with the fact that in the circle of my peers ... amongst Working Gurus, I am known as a ... a dum-dum. I am obliged to tell you of certain miracles performed by me where small ironies intruded, and the results were ... unfortunate."

Jackie grabbed him again by the lapels of his silk vest. Two buttons popped off. "I don't care," Jackie said. "I want the miracle."

Chatterje gulped. "Indeed. And you shall have it. But first — my faith dictates this candor. There was a wrestling promoter in Vero Beach, Florida, who wanted to take an ocean trip. That was *his* dream. I booked him passage on the *Andrea Doria*."

"I wanna make people laugh," Jackie said.

"I have in mind," Chatterje said, as if Jackie weren't in the room, "another ill-starred situation. Having to do with a retired schoolteacher lady in Spokane, Washington. A Civil War buff. An admirer of the Great Emancipator. Wanted only one thing. To be in Lincoln's Cabinet." He closed his eyes. "Wound up in an asylum, claiming she was a sock with 'G.A.R.' embroidered along her side — and had to be restrained from sticking darning needles into her head."

"I just wanna make people laugh," Jackie repeated, like a record needle caught in a groove. "Laugh — understand?"

"I had a transaction," Chatterje said, "with an elderly man in Los Angeles. Seventy-one years old. He had been forced to give up the act of love because of a cessation of male powers. We transacted for one glorious moment in which he might once again rise to the occasion." Chatterje looked off mournfully. "It occurred at a large Kiwanis banquet in front of a mixed audience of a thousand people while he was making a speech on 'Communists Cause Depression.' He actually lifted the speaker's table and spilled all the desserts. And as to finding a partner worthy of his ardor — that was quite impossible. Most of the women had fainted."

"I don't give a damn," Jackie said. "I wanna make people laugh!"

"But am I getting through to you, Mr. Slater? There are miracles ... and there are risks."

The dream still hovered. "I'll take the risk," Jackie said. "Just go ahead and do it!"

Chatterje looked up toward the ceiling, closed his eyes, whispered something under his breath, then smiled. "It is done," he said.

"What's done?" Jackie asked.

The bartender stood at the door, then suddenly smiled and then laughed. "What's done?" he said. "Did you get that? What's done?" He began to laugh, and stood there, laughing even louder.

Jackie walked over to him and gaped. "What did I say?" he asked.

The bartender screamed with laughter. "What did he say! Oh, Jesus — you knock me out. I swear — you knock me out!" He bent over double, catching his breath, as the laughter rolled out of him.

Jackie turned and looked across at Chatterje. "I think you've done it," he said, as the dream floated down to embrace him. "Guru! You've done it! You've made the miracle."

The bartender sent out another spasm of laughter.

Chatterje smiled, swallowed, and tiptoed across the room past the shrieking bartender. He opened the front door, then turned and looked over his shoulder. "All things are possible."

He walked out into the streets, but paused long enough to look through the window at the convulsed bartender and Jackie standing there, bemused and bewildered. Chatterje closed his eyes, then slowly opened them and looked skyward. "Oh, Great Guru," he said reverently to the black canopy above him. "I have wrought another miracle. Please ... in your infinite compassion ... don't make this as piss-poor as all the others!"

On the following Tuesday he filled in for a barker on a roadshow outside of Syracuse and barely escaped a mob of concessionaires who were of a mind to beat the hell out of him. His pitch had drawn ninety percent of the audience away from everything else on the Midway. And while three hundred people screamed their laughter at him, the rest of the show died. Nobody looked at the freaks, played the games of chance, checked out the dancing girls, or bought the cotton candy. They stood there, elbow to rib cage, convulsing at the little fat man on the stand whose every gesture sent them into explosive gales of uncontrollable hilarity.

The carny owner gave him a week's pay, which he drank up by the next night. But he also gave him the name of a nightclub owner in New Rochelle. Jackie played that roadhouse beginning on a Friday night. By the following Wednesday, it was SRO in a club whose audience up to that point couldn't have supplied a ten-man minyan on the night of the Armistice.

It kept going.

He played the Copacabana in New York for a week's booking and a three-week holdover. Then he went on the *Ed Sullivan Show* and broke all precedents by being asked to come back on three weeks in a row.

He filled in for Johnny Carson on the *Tonight Show*. And NBC offered him twenty bills a week to do his own show.

His humor remained the same: Ancient. And he was constant: Fat, ungainly, ugly. But people laughed.

A year passed. He was playing the Dunes in Vegas when Jules Kettleman returned and walked into his dressing room between shows, looking like a runaway mongrel a step ahead of a dog catcher.

"Hey, Jackie," Jules said sorrowfully as he entered the sumptuous dressing room, "I've been out front. You killed 'em. Honest to God, Jackie, you killed 'em. I hope ... I hope you understood why I had to cop out."

It was then he realized that Jackie was barely listening to him. He sat at his dressing table, staring at the letters and telegrams. Then the fat man looked up. "I always kill 'em, Julie. I fracture 'em. I lay 'em out."

"You're fantastic," Jules whispered. He took a step over and put his hands on Jackie's sloping shoulders. "I ... I was proud of you, Jackie."

"What about the steel-guitar band?"

"Played a Fair date in Columbus, Ohio. They got booed off the stage." Jules closed his eyes. "I didn't have no choice in that, Jackie. I hadda take on somebody else — or starve."

Jackie reached up and patted Jules's fingers. "Forget it," Jackie said. "I understand." Then he folded his hands in front of him on the dressing table. "What I don't understand," he said softly, "is why I'm not getting any kicks."

"Whaddya mean, Jackie?"

"I mean ... I'm boffo. No matter what I do ... what I say ... I open my mouth and everybody goes ape. They fall down. I tell a gag that's got spider webs on it. I don't mean just *old*, Julie — I mean like a collector's item. And the people roll on the floor."

"That's great, Jackie."

Jackie turned to him. "It should be," he said tremulously. "It *should* be great. But it isn't, Jules. It isn't at all. It's —" He struggled for a word. "Dull. That's what the hell it is. It's dull."

Jules took a step back and looked around the paneled room. "Isn't that what you want?" he asked. "To make people laugh?"

Jackie nodded.

"Isn't that what you're doing?"

Again Jackie nodded.

"I seen the *Variety* review when you did the *Carol Burnett Show*. It said you broke up the joint."

Again Jackie turned to him. "I broke up the joint. You wanna know how I broke up the joint? I walked out in front of the camera — and I took my hat off. That's it. I took my hat off. They screamed. They fell down. Then ... at the end of the show, I put my hat back on. You shoulda heard 'em. I haven't had laughs like that since they used to push me off the dock."

Jackie looked at his reflection in the mirror. "Julie —" he said softly.

"Yeah, Jackie?"

"I'm bored. I know it don't make any sense — but I'm bored. It used to be I had to work for it. Fight for it. Kill myself for it. And now ..." He closed his eyes. "Now it's dullsville."

Jules stared at him. "Whaddya want, Jackie? I mean — you alla time wanted to make people laugh. Well, that's what's happened. What more do you want? A comic wants to get laughs."

Jackie got to his feet. Two hundred and eighty pounds of blubber, suet, accordion flesh. "That don't do it, Julie," he said positively. "Laughs aren't enough. *Anybody* can get laughs. A fat little Yo-Yo kid gets pushed off a dock. So, big deal — they laugh."

He paced back and forth across the room. "There's gotta be something more. A guy can't go through life just tickling people. A guy's gotta be more than just a clown." He paused by the table and grabbed for a fistful of letters and telegrams. "Looka these! Telegrams. Letters. Cables. Deals. Offers. Guarantees. But to do *what?*" He waved them in the air. "To be a rum-dum, baggy pants, horse's ass of a nitwit — well, I'll tell you something, Julie —"

He stopped in midair, staring down at a telegram in his hand. The other papers fluttered to the floor.

"What is it, Jackie?" Jules asked.

Jackie handed him the telegram. "Read that," he said.

Jules took the telegram and read it, then looked up, his intense little face mildly questioning. "Who's Daniel Merrill?" he asked.

Jackie ripped the telegram from his hand. "Jules," he said, his voice shaking, "you've gotta get outta the tent show. You gotta forget the carnival. You wanna handle donickers and rag-bag operators all your life?" He held up the telegram in his fist. "This is legit! This is Broadway!" He looked down at the telegram and read aloud. " 'Would like to discuss with you the possibility of your playing a straight dramatic role in play I have under option —' " Then he slowly lowered the telegram and stared out at nothing across the room. "A passport to greatness — and there it sits on my dressing table. Julie — you dig? *A straight dramatic role!* Me! Jackie Slater! An actor!"

Jules scratched his jaw. "Jackie," he said somberly, "you never done no acting. You was never a straight man. You're a comic."

Jackie looked at him almost pityingly over the middle roll of a triple chin. "*Was* a comic," he said softly. "*Was* a clown. *Was* a joker. *Was* a funny man. *Was* a dolt, clod, dunce, klutz! But no more! Understand? No more! Jack Slater." He paused for a moment, looked up at the ceiling. "Make that John Slater."

He moved to a position in front of the mirror and looked at himself with a raised eyebrow. "Jonathon Slater."

Another dream was building. He wasn't in the dressing room. He was in the Santa Monica Civic Auditorium. There were three thousand people in the place — and not a sound.

"For the best actor," Jackie said in somber tones, "in a leading role — the envelope, please. And the winner is —"

Fireworks. Sky rockets. Bursting lights across the sky. The dream. The *new* dream. There goes Jackie Slater, Ma. Oh, God, what a man. What an incredible actor. What a brilliant talent.

The readings were held in a drafty, semidark Fifty-eighth Street theater.

Five rows back from the proscenium sat the director, the producer, and a couple of the show's backers.

On the stage a few actors lolled around, reading scripts. One or two of them looked at Jackie, who stood in their midst waiting expectantly.

The director leaned forward in his seat from the audience. "Page one of Act Two, Mr. Slater — from the top. Just keep in mind that you're a circus clown. You've just discovered that your wife has left you. You've just read her note, and at this moment there isn't a single thing on earth you want to live for."

"Right," Jackie said breathlessly, "right — I got it."

"Miss Wilson," the director called to a girl standing a few feet away on the stage. "Play the girl acrobat, if you will."

The pretty mini-skirted girl walked over to stand next to Jackie, carrying her script. She looked up toward the director, who nodded.

"What's the matter, Bozo?" the girl read from the script. "You look odd."

Jackie cleared his throat and unbuttoned the middle button of a shrieking houndstooth sport coat. "Sure," he announced in stentorian tones, "I'm odd. I'm a clown. A clown is supposed to look odd. But a funny thing happened to me on the way over to the circus. My life just got dissolved."

He closed his eyes and put a fist to his forehead and let out a short, strangled sob.

One of the actors chuckled. Another actor blew out his laughter after holding it back for a moment. One of the backers in the theater seats let out a loud, cackling giggle.

Jackie looked down at his script again. "A clown isn't supposed to cry," he said, putting a wavering quality to his voice. "A clown is supposed to laugh. Ha-ha-ha."

The director in the audience began to smile. Merrill, alongside, laughed softly. And after a moment, everyone in the theater was laughing.

Jackie had to shout to make his next line heard. "But the smiles are hand painted." He made a gesture of applying paint to his mouth.

That did it.

No more reading.

No more anything.

Only laughter. A thunderous, rolling, shrieking laughter.

The director turned to Merrill. "I'm sorry, Mr. Merrill," he said through his laughter, "the guy's a comic. No matter what he reads — it comes out like a gag."

Merrill nodded and scratched his moustache, wiping the tears off his own cheeks as he did so. "I thought he was what we needed," he said. "Something … something about his face —"

"His face!" The director shrieked and laughed again. "His face, gestures, everything — is for laughs." He looked back toward Jackie on the stage and convulsed. "Look at him," he shrieked. "Will you look at him?"

Jackie just stood there, script in hand, his pudgy little face screwed up like a child about to cry. And around him the laughter surged.

Merrill continued to wipe the tears from his cheeks and turned to the director. "I made a mistake," he said. "Shake his hand, pat his back, and get him the hell out of here."

The director nodded, rose, and carried his laughter with him to the aisle and then down to the foot of the stage. "I'm sorry, Mr. Slater," he began.

Jackie glared at him over the footlights, then looked briefly around him. His voice drowned out the laughter. "You wanna know something?" Jackie shouted.

Very gradually the laughter faded into silence.

"I'll tell you something," Jackie said. "You're dirty, rotten people is what you are! You're dirty, rotten, insensitive people! You're the kind … you're the kind who would push a kid off a dock — that's what you'd do!"

More silence. Then the director screamed with laughter. "Push him off a dock," he said, the laughter gurgling and bubbling inside of him. "Push him off a dock."

They were all laughing … and they couldn't stop as Jackie wrapped his dignity around him like a cloak and stalked off the stage.

Chatterje was out in the alley when Jackie came out the stage-door exit. He was sitting on a garbage can, looking as ratty and poverty-stricken as ever. The cracked red ruby reflected the glint of a dying afternoon sun. He surveyed Jackie sadly.

"As must be obvious, yefendi," he said in his fluty little voice, "miracles are not without risks … unforeseen little addenda."

Jackie lumbered over to him. "Unforeseen little addenda," he repeated, his features working, "like spending the rest of my life tickling people. Lemme tell you something, you half-pint guru — I can't say 'Good morning' …. 'How are you?' … 'A glass of orange juice, please,' without people laughing at me."

Chatterje seemed to shrivel. "It was as you wished," he said in a whisper.

"Well, I don't wish it now!" Jackie shouted at him. "I've had it with the boffos. I want another miracle. You understand? You dig, you motheaten Gunga Din, you? I want you to fix it so that nobody *ever* laughs at me again."

Chatterje unfolded his skinny little toothpick legs and got off the garbage can. He looked stricken. "Yefendi," he said apologetically, "there is an unwritten law. One miracle to a customer. And as must be obvious with me and my miracles — this should be an occasion for you to count your blessings!"

Jackie thrust out a big hambone arm and lifted Chatterje off his feet. "You listen to me, you second-rate swami, you — I want another miracle. I want people to cry when I talk — not laugh. So you make that happen, or they'll be able to wrap up what's left of you in that Ace bandage you wear around your head and deposit you in a quart can." He shook Chatterje. "You hear me? You wilted wizard, you — make another miracle."

Chatterje clawed at Jackie's hands until he removed them. He stood there for a few silent moments, then looked skyward and mumbled some soundless words; then mournfully he turned back to Jackie. "It is done," he said.

"Done?" Jackie asked suspiciously.

"Done," Chatterje answered. "You will never again be laughed at, yefendi. Never ever. Never, never ever!"

Chatterje took a quick step backward as Jackie moved closer to him.

"You sure?" Jackie asked.

Chatterje touched his forehead. "I am as certain of this, yefendi, as I am that my peers are quite correct." The corners of his mouth turned down. "As a guru, I am a dismal, abject, altogether substandard klutz. A failure, yefendi. That is what I am."

Jackie glared at him. "We'll see," he said. "We'll just see."

He took his fat man's walk to the opening of the alley, then looked across the street, where a shriveled old woman sold flowers from a battered kiosk. "Hey," Jackie shouted at her. "Hey, lady! Ever hear the one about the two Arabs who got on the streetcar?"

The old woman looked at him, startled.

Jackie stepped off the curb. "Well, this one Arab says to the other Arab —"

Chatterje screamed.

The old woman shut her eyes.

The cab driver went cold all over as he tried to jam on the brake.

There was the sound of a thud and a squish, and then two funny sounds, like twin balloons being punctured as the wheels rolled over Jackie Slater's body.

Pedestrians stood transfixed, staring at the motionless, twisted body of the fat man in the middle of the street.

Moments later there came the sound of an approaching siren.

There were the shocked murmurings of the onlookers.

But no laughter. No laughter at all.

The flower lady cried. Tears rolled down her cheeks and dropped like little liquid petals onto the bunches of violets.

Chatterje's little black shoe-button eyes took in everything. He let his gaze rest on the sobbing flower lady, then toward Jackie Slater's body. Laughter wasn't enough for you, yefendi, he thought to himself. No, indeed — tears you wanted. He took a deep breath and moved in the opposite direction down the street. "It's a moot question," he said to the pink-and-orange-sunset sky. "An altogether moot question."

The thin little sounds of the flower lady faded off, and in their place came the ear-splitting din of the ambulance's siren.

"Shall I continue the miracle route? Shall I perhaps open up a restaurant featuring curried delicacies, or perhaps a sabbatical while I brush up on the guru art?"

Chatterje took a last look at the body of Jackie Slater being lifted onto a stretcher and smiled sadly. "Poor yefendi," he whispered. "At least you have no more choices to make."

Then he continued down the sidewalk, as once again the ambulance's siren sent out its wailing notice of departure, and the big white vehicle disappeared around the corner carrying two hundred and eighty pounds of a late comedian.

PAMELA'S VOICE

It had been an absolutely smashing day, begun auspiciously with his favorite eggs-Benedict breakfast, which he prepared himself, and then washed down with a dainty, exquisite Pinot. He had tiptoed quietly from the house for a brisk and invigorating walk in the clear April morning and then returned before Pamela had awakened. Then he had strung the piano wire across the third step from the top of the stairway, testing it for strength and tautness. Following that, he'd fixed himself a spot of Irish coffee in the study and sat patiently in his favorite leather chair facing the bay window that offered such a delightful view of the incredibly beautiful morning.

At promptly eleven o'clock the bell from Pamela's bedroom began to jangle furiously. He had smiled, picturing her in her hair net, mud pack, chin strap, and all the other nocturnal devices Pamela used to give battle to encroaching age.

He sipped at his coffee, hearing the groaning wheeze of the mattress as she left the bed, and then her heavy footsteps to the door, followed by her shrill voice calling his name as she came out onto the upper landing.

"Jonathan? Jonathan, are you down there? Jonathan, why aren't you answering my —"

From the study he heard first her surprised gasp and then her throttled scream. Close behind was a loud thump, and then more thumps as Pamela had come somersaulting down the stairs, her heavy body picking up momentum, until she had finished her journey on the hard oak floor at the foot of the stairs.

Jonathan came out of the study, to find her sitting upright against the wall in a welter of silk bathrobe and hanging hair net directly under the severe-looking portrait of her great-grandfather. Her broken neck, rooster-style, left her shoulderblades at an impossible angle; and when Jonathan gently lifted up her head, her still-open eyes, smudged with mascara, glared at him with silent fury under the arched, plucked eyebrows. He had gazed into the dead horse face of his wife, through the cracks of the mud pack and the various creams, and noted that in death, as in life, Pamela was perhaps the ugliest woman on the face of the earth.

But it was odd, he thought, as he walked to the phone to perform the meaningless ritual of calling a doctor, that even in death her mouth was open. There was that yawning cavern with the big yellow teeth, frozen in its accustomed position — parted and agape. He could imagine what was clogged up by the sudden detour in her windpipe — her daily epithets, criticisms, whinings, and multiple angers, precipitously cut off by Jonathan's piano wire.

The burnished mahogany casket reflected the four tall candles as well as the tiers of flowers and wreaths placed around it. And Jonathan, his spare, trim little frame housed impeccably in a silk smoking jacket, sat in his leather chair across the room looking at it. He placed a long cigarette in a holder, lit it, started to put the match into an ashtray, and then, as if reminded by the casket, flipped the match onto the carpet. He then tapped the ashes off his cigarette to land at his feet and leaned back luxuriously. Among the myriad things that Pamela had disapproved of, smoking was near the top of the list. And dropping ashes on the carpet, she had placed in the same category as child beating and infidelity. But there were many things, Jonathan reflected, that Pamela had disapproved of. The candles, Jonathan noted, made the Victorian room brighter than it ever had been. Pamela had lectured him incessantly about wasting electricity. She would walk from room to room, turning off light switches. "When not in use — turn off the juice," she would say. And then she would move into whatever room Jonathan was in and sniff the air. "Have you been smoking, Jonathan?" she would always ask. "Tobacco is one of the most miserable poisons extant. Quite apart from what it does to the body — it fouls the air permanently."

Jonathan smiled as he reflected. Pamela had never known what "permanently" meant until she'd been placed in the box across the room. Pamela had really not known much of anything except how to rage, persecute, complain, and vilify. Jonathan had wished for her death for the first five years, desperately prayed for it for the next five, and actively planned it for the last five. Fifteen years, he thought to himself, fifteen years with Pamela's mouth — that working, smacking, perpetually moving noise box that kept opening and shutting as if on an oiled hinge, giving him no peace, no silence, no escape.

He rose from the chair, dusted some ashes off the lapel of his smoking jacket, and walked over to a small cabinet. From it he took out a bottle of wine that he had formerly hidden in the cellar. He squinted at its label. A light-bodied claret from 1923, which, Jonathan reflected again, had been a fair year. He carried the bottle back over to the chair, and in the process passed Pamela sitting on the sofa. He nodded affably toward her, then stopped in his tracks as a glacier rose from his feet and took a freezing journey up to his brain. Pamela! Pamela sitting on the sofa. He blinked, swallowed, then turned very slowly to look again toward the sofa.

Pamela sat there, slightly transparent and very ghost-like. But she sat there. And there was nothing ephemeral in the voice. It was Pamela's — shrill, grating, enveloping. "Nothing better to do tonight, Jonathan? Just stand there like a bump on a log?"

Jonathan blinked again and stared.

"Look hard enough, and you'll see me. You're blind as a bat, Jonathan."

Jonathan checked the bottle in his hand to see if perhaps he had already drunk from it. It was still corked and full. He took a deep breath. "Pamela? Is that your voice?"

The specter on the sofa seemed to grow more solid. "Whose voice were you expecting, you idiot? Who else's voice could it possibly be? And don't stand there gaping like an owl."

Jonathan sat down in his favorite chair. Of course, it was Pamela. No one else could fire off that many tired metaphors per minute. And no one's voice could sound like a fingernail across a blackboard like Pamela's.

He carefully put the bottle aside, then forced himself to look directly at Pamela. Yes, it was definitely Pamela. The severe, hating eyes — the long tallow-colored face — the gaping open mouth.

"Surprised?" Pamela asked.

"At what?"

The figure on the sofa shrugged. "At my being here."

Jonathan leaned back in the chair. He felt no fear at all. Pamela, the dead apparition, seemed infinitely less menacing than Pamela — that shrewish, piano-legged bane of fifteen endless years.

"Hardly surprised," he said mildly. "In life, my dear Pamela, you arrived every place uninvited. You and that hyena-mating voice of yours."

She seemed totally materialized now, and sat as she had always sat — hunched forward, hands clenched into fists, an open mouth twisted like the bent mouthpiece of a bugle.

"Tell me, Pamela," he said, "how *are* things up there? Keeping you occupied, are they? Keeping you contented? Are there lives — or rather, *after*lives — you can destroy with gossip? Reputations you can filthy up with your dark little suspicions and that kitchen-knife tongue of yours?" He laughed. "Incredible. Really incredible. It never occurred to me, Pamela." He pointed at her. "You're probably not even up there. Most likely you're —" He stopped, pointing a finger at the floor.

"Crazy as a loon," Pamela said. "I'm neither, Jonathan. I'm right here. I've not left, though you did your level best to get me out of the way."

Jonathan looked over at the casket and smiled. "Pamela," he said, "you *are* out of the way. Resilient, you were. But altogether mortal. And being mortal, my dear, a broken neck did you in nicely." He leaned forward in the chair. "Was it painful? I mean, when you landed at the foot of the stairs — hurt much, did it?"

"Not a particle," Pamela said icily.

"Pity." Jonathan shook his head a little forlornly. "That rather takes the fun out of it. I'd hoped the discomfort would be somewhat prolonged. You know — tit for tat. My fifteen-odd years of marital agony — against at least a few minutes of some pronounced pain of your own. A real pity, Pamela."

Pamela rose from the sofa. "You had it rough, you did," she screeched at him. "You meandering tomcat, you! Why, I could have had my pick of any man in town! My daddy, God rest his soul, had to bar the doors to keep the swains from forcing their way in."

Jonathan looked up at the ceiling and laughed. "The swains?" he roared. "The swains, indeed. My God, Pamela, they weren't swains. They were a two-platoon system of fortune-hunters and hungry gigolos!"

"So *you* say!"

"Because it's the truth. Without your big daddy's bank account, you couldn't have gotten a proposal in an all-male penal colony. You couldn't have even gotten an indecent proposition!"

"Now, you listen to me, Jonathan." Her shrill voice, just as always, enveloped the room.

Jonathan simply turned away and lit another cigarette. "I have listened to you, Pamela," he said quietly, "for over fifteen years. I have listened to you to the point of a bleeding ulcer, two ruptured eardrums, and a permanent migraine!"

With this he uncorked the wine bottle, then started to carry it back over to the chest for a glass. Inexplicably, Pamela was standing in front of him. He hadn't seen her move. She just appeared, as if transported from her former place to a point in front of the chest directly in Jonathan's path. He stopped and drew away from her waggling finger.

"You listen to me, Jonathan," she said, "and you keep listening, because I intend to keep right on talking."

Jonathan shrugged, turned, and retreated back to his chair. Once again he found Pamela standing in front of him, blocking him.

"You were a swine as a husband." Her voice, a constant, perpetual siren shrilled at him, and he found himself staring at that omniscient cave that kept opening and closing. "You were a rotter as a companion — a faithless fancy Dan with all the morals of a Bowery wino!"

Then something exploded inside of him. That mouth of hers … that voice of hers clawed a hole in his restraint, and through it poured out all the rage, all the frustration, all the mountainous hatred he had managed to throttle over the miserable decade and a half.

"You bloody bitch, you!" he screamed at her. "Close that big flapping mouth of yours! You think I've risked an electric chair just to suffer *more* of you? That suet-pudding body of yours — that's one thing. But that voice of yours, Pamela — that voice! That untuned trombone screech that fills the room every time you air your tonsils!"

It flowed out of him — the hot, bubbling waves of venom so long pent up. "That's what made me do it, Pamela. That cacophony of noise — that off-key lunch whistle — that cracked calliope that woke me in the morning and shrieked at me throughout the day and battered my head at night!"

He held out a fist in front of her face. "*That's* why I murdered you, Pamela. *So I wouldn't have to listen to that voice of yours!*"

Pamela's laughter filled the room and made him wince.

"Well, now," she said, "fancy that! Poor, sensitive man with the delicate ears! Didn't care for the sound of my voice."

She sauntered back over to the sofa and sat down. "And what do you suppose you're listening to now, Jonathan?" she asked. "Dead, I may be — but what is it you're listening to?"

Jonathan moved over to the casket and leaned against it, again lighting a cigarette. "What am I listening to?" he repeated. He tapped his forehead. "My imagination. That's what I'm listening to. I'm listening, Pamela, to a fantasy. I'm looking at a specter. You — that dumpy, flabby carcass of yours — that pulsating and perpetual nagging — *I'm imagining it!*"

He let the fingers of one hand move across the polished surface of the casket. "Do you recall what Scrooge said to the ghost of Marley?" he asked her. " 'You may be an undigested bit of beef, a blot of mustard, a crumb of cheese, a fragment of an undone potato. There is more of gravy than grave about you.' Understand, Pamela? You're very likely part of my eggs Benedict — simply a case of stereophonic indigestion!"

He smiled, tapped the side of the casket, then crooked a finger at her. "Why fight it, Pamela? It's beddy-bye time. Permanent beddy-bye time." He looked at his watch. "They'll be coming for you soon."

Pamela's voice sounded puzzled. "Who will?"

"Why, the funeral director and his minions, of course. We're going to convey you to the cemetery."

Pamela stared at him. "How's that again, Jonathan?"

Jonathan's anger fizzled out like a spent firecracker. His voice was patient. "The cemetery, my dear. The repository of the deceased. The tomb ... the vault ... the crypt ... the resting place ... the ossuary. Dig? Boot Hill, baby."

Pamela sighed. "I swear, Jonathan. You're still the most absent-minded man I ever met. Absentminded as a professor."

"I am?" he said, pointing to himself.

"Don't you remember? You buried me months ago."

Jonathan blinked at her. "I did *what?*" he asked, feeling a funny disorientation.

"I fell down the stairs," Pamela said, "on the seventeenth of April. My funeral was on the nineteenth. And this is August."

Again he blinked at her and tried to remember. How could it be August? The whole thing had happened just that morning. Or had it? He suddenly realized that he was unable to piece together the chronology of the day. He remembered his walk and the eggs Benedict and the piano wire. But was that this morning? Or another day? Or when was it?

"August?" he repeated.

"August," she answered in an unusually soft voice.

He stared at her for a long moment, took a few steps halfway across the room toward her, then stopped and looked over his shoulder at the casket, jerking his thumb at it. "And ... that?" he asked, whispering.

He didn't wait for her reply. He turned and walked back over to the casket, feeling the anchor-chain weight of premonition — not wanting to look — but compelled to look, even so.

Pamela folded her arms in front of her. When she spoke, her voice zoomed up to its normal high-pitched, shattering decibel level. "You've only yourself to blame," she bugled out triumphantly. "It's no more than you deserve for so excessively celebrating my demise."

Jonathan peered into the casket. The cigarette and its holder fell to the floor.

Lying there, on tufted velvet, was himself — hands folded in peaceful repose.

Pamela's voice formed an obligato to the silent moment. "All that rich food," she scolded, "those late hours, the alcoholic spirits. If

I'd told you once, I'd told you a hundred times, Jonathan. You were constitutionally unsuited to the life of indecency and Bacchanalian self-indulgence."

Jonathan stood there, rooted — staring in numb disbelief at his own waxen face in the casket. He was only barely conscious of the fractious screech that came from across the room.

"Would you listen to me, Jonathan? Of course not. Like all the other sound advice I offered you down through the years, you ungratefully ignored it! And don't think I don't know why you married me, you fortune-hunting finagler. You married me for my money, my position, my family, this house —"

Jonathan tore his gaze away from the corpse and turned back toward Pamela. "Pamela," he said, "it isn't just you ... it's also —"

Pamela filled it in for him. "You, Jonathan. Quite correct. The word is 'ghost.' That's precisely what you are."

What an incredibly strange dream, Jonathan thought to himself as he moved back over to the chair. Nightmare on top of nightmare.

He found her at his elbow. "I reject that," he announced in a slightly quavering voice, "as palpably impossible. I reject you, Pamela. Because when one dies — one either goes up there" — he pointed to the ceiling — "or down there." He pointed to the floor.

"You're right as rain, Jonathan," Pamela said. "Right as rain. And in heaven you can do anything you want. Now, my being a social woman, an extrovert, you might say — a person who enjoys communicating — well, I shall spend the rest of my eternity talking. And you, Jonathan — you pusher of wives down staircases — while I talk through eternity ... you'll *listen*."

Again he found himself staring at her mouth. "Eternity?" he whispered. He pointed to himself. "Me?" He pointed to her. "Listening to you?"

Someplace deep within him he accepted. He knew. It was no nightmare. At least it was no sleeping nightmare. This nightmare lived and breathed and existed.

He cleared his throat. "That's grossly unfair, Pamela," he announced. "You just said that in heaven one can do anything one wishes."

Pamela's beady lizard eyes shone with triumphant pleasure. "In heaven, Jonathan — indeed. But I'm afraid the organization to which *you've* been assigned is not quite so accommodating."

And he knew. Oh, yes, indeed — he knew. He remembered his death then, as he remembered hers. The sharp pain in his chest, the clammy wetness of his gray skin seen in the bedroom mirror as he fell forward against it, and watched the ceiling converge with walls as he landed on the floor. His death was a matter of record, and he knew it. And he knew something else. Pamela was quite correct. No theological abstraction here. Not angels and devils. Not clouds and brimstone pits. Eternity was tailored for the individual. And as he watched her mouth move and heard the staccato, ceaseless, remorseless, unending shrillness of her voice, he knew all about *his* eternity.

"Now, what was I saying?" Pamela asked. "Oh, yes. As I was commenting before, Jonathan, just before you pushed me down those stairs — it's always been my feeling that you can judge a man by the way he listens."

Jonathan stood there helplessly, hopelessly. His ears began to twitch and burn. His head began to ache.

And still Pamela's voice continued. "Not the way a man dresses, Jonathan. Mind you, that's important. It's the way a man listens. Now, if a man is responsive … if he's attentive … if a man really has an interest in what you're saying —"

The grandfather clock in the corner of the room ticked away in perfect cadence to Pamela's voice. Tick-tick-tick.

"And, Jonathan, I want to discuss something else with you —"

Tick-tick-tick.

"This cigarette-smoking thing. You know that tobacco is a miserable poison. And it fouls up the air."

Tick-tick-tick.

"And another thing, Jonathan —"

Tick-tick-tick.

The wave of noise smashed over his brain like pounding surf. He felt a wetness and looked down at the tears on his transparent hands. There were two things he knew for certain. Ghosts could cry.

"Now, let me tell you this, Jonathan —"

And ghosts could hear.

The grandfather clock and Pamela's voice went on ... and on ... and on ....

DOES THE NAME GRIMSBY
DO ANYTHING TO YOU?

For the second time that night, he had the Dream. Once again he was in Falcon, heading downward toward the surface of the moon. The voice of Capcom, 200,000 miles away, filtered into his earphones.

"Houston, you're go for landing. Over."

Aloud, in his dark bedroom, Lt. Commander Jonathan Cornelius Evans relived the moment. "Roger, understand. Go for landing. 3,000 feet," he said aloud.

"Copy," Capcom responded.

The voices jumbled together. A mental mosaic of memory. And his own voice continued to document the descent. "We're go. Hang tight. We're go. 2,000 feet. 2,000 feet into the AGS. 47 degrees. 35 degrees. 750, coming down at 23. 700 feet, 21 down. 33 degrees. 600 feet, down at 19. 540 feet, down at 30 — down at 15. 400 feet, down at 9."

And the Dream went on. A Xerox copy of the way it had been. Just the way it had been. Falcon, the lunar module, on its way to the moon. With Lt. Commander Evans at the controls.

Alongside of him his wife stirred and opened her eyes, turned toward the sleeping face and the mumbled monologue.

His voice went on. "Lights on. Down 2½. Forward. Forward. Good. 40 feet, down 2½. Picking up some dust. 30 feet, 2½ down. Faint shadow. 4 forward. 4 forward, dipping to the right a little. 6."

Monica Evans, now wideawake, looked through the darkness at the silhouetted face of her husband and wished she might enter that dream or whatever it was — whatever was that recurring night journey he traveled each night since his return.

But Lt. Commander Evans was on the moon.

"Contact light. Okay, engines stopped. ACA out of detent. Modes control both auto, descent engine command override off. Engine arm, off. 413 is in."

"We copy you down, Falcon," said Capcom.

He was there on the surface of the moon, the panel of red lights in front of him glowing in the darkness of the little cabin.

"Houston, Tranquillity base here. Falcon has landed. Repeat. Falcon has landed."

His wife watched him as he slowly rose to a sitting position in the bed, his eyes now wide open, staring across the room at the dresser mirror. She tried to look at his eyes as if in their vision might be something to be shared. But the eyes eluded her. They were looking out of a small circular window, clouded and pitted, but revealing the surface of the moon. The incredibly black sky. The lonely, virgin nothingness of the cratered landscape outside.

And then, in the manner of dreams, time was telescoped. He stood on the top rung of the ladder and heard Capcom's voice in his earphones.

"Okay, Jonny, we can see you coming down the ladder now."

"Okay," he said. "I just checked — getting back up to that first step. It's not even collapsed too far, but it's adequate to get back up."

"Roger, we copy," said Capcom.

Slowly he turned his head in the little glass-cubed world of his space helmet and looked down. His heavily encased feet started down the ladder, touching each rung as he moved.

"I'm at the foot of the ladder," he said. "The LM foot pads are only depressed in the surface ... about one or two inches. The surface appears to be very, very fine-grained as you get close to it. It's almost like powder. Now and then, it's very fine."

There was a silence then. A silence of the space night spread out from the moon to the earth; the silence of that earth waiting, staring up at the golden disk and marveling that it had been reached and was now being occupied; the tense silence of the collective bated breaths of the thousands of technicians hunched over panels and viewing devices and screens.

Then Lt. Commander Evans took the final step, and first one foot and then the other touched the surface.

Aloud he said, "I'm on the moon." But to himself — a roaring, exulting thing rippled through him. The first! He was the first! Nobody before him. Nobody ahead of him. The first!

His wife listened to the changed cadence of his breathing. The garbled sounds were irregular and faster, and she thought she caught the word "first."

Then, at this point, as it had for weeks, he turned quiet. He just sat there on the bed, eyes wide open, but saying nothing further. This was the part of the Dream that mystified her. He drew a curtain over this part. But in his mind ... in his sleeping mind, this was the most vivid. Carrying the brass plaque across the powdery terrain in the strange, too-bright illumination of the module spotlights. And he was about to place it down on the surface of the moon. Man's claim to outer space. Officially designated by the President of the United States and so written on the plaque.

"Here men from the planet Earth first set foot upon the Moon. July, 1969. A. D. We came in peace for all mankind." And signed by the President of the United States. He remembered looking down at that fragment of dusty ground where he would place the plaque.

And then he woke up.

"Grimsby." This came aloud from his mouth — suddenly lifted out in clarity from the rest of the mumbling. "Grimsby." He repeated it.

His wife reached out and touched his perspiring cheek. "Jonny? Jonny, are you all right?"

He turned to her, his eyes now seeing. He was back on earth. Back at his house. Back in his bedroom. He now saw walls and a dresser mirror and the silhouetted lovely form of his wife's face in the darkness. His pajama top clung to his soggy body like some kind of massive leech.

"What's the matter?" he asked her.

She kept staring at him. "Grimsby," she said.

He blinked at her. "Grimsby? What about Grimsby?"

"That's the name you just said, Jonny. Grimsby."

He just stared at her. He couldn't focus. The name hung out there in front of him like a giant mobile.

"Grimsby," he murmured. "Grimsby." He shook his head. "I'll be damned if I know where that name came from."

Then he got out of the bed, walked over to the dresser, felt around for some cigarettes, got one and lit it, then turned to her. "Want a smoke?"

She shook her head, watching the little flare of match light and then the red glow at the end of the cigarette.

"You've had a dream every night, Jonny. Every night since you've come back."

She felt his smile in the dark room.

He moved back toward the bed and sat down, reaching out to touch her. Through the silk of her nightgown he felt her tremble. "What have I been saying in my sleep?" he asked her. "Incriminating names of broads?" He laughed.

She reached up and took his hand, holding tight to it. "You never dreamed before," she said. "You *never* talked in your sleep."

He laughed — that rich, warm, male laugh of his. "Honey," he said, "I never took a walk on the moon before."

She looked at his face as he turned away, seeing the outline of the profile illuminated in the cigarette light — thoughtful now, reflective.

"You know something?" he said softly. "No matter what happens — it's in the book. That one they can't take away from me. I was the first."

She looked at his silhouette — that familiar jutting iron jaw, the deep-set, searching eyes, the strength of the man. She's always felt an exciting, throbbing pride in her husband. There was not (though she would never admit this even to herself) so much passion in the marriage as there was a respect. She had married courage and will and dedication. Jonny Evans had worn a white uniform on their wedding day. Jonny Evans had never discarded that uniform through eleven years of marriage. No, there had not been much passion, but there had always been gentleness. And there had always been sharing. Until ... and this was suddenly part of her vague fear ... until Apollo. Until she had looked at him on the television screen and seen him lifted onto the deck of the carrier. So incredibly triumphant. And even then — in those first moments — against a background of television cameras, White House luncheons, worldwide adulation — some disquieting thing had taken hold. Not just his intensity — he had always been intense. And not just his preoccupation — this had always been a part of Jonny Evans. When he tested a jet; when he first joined the astronaut program; during all those long months, preparing for the landing on the moon. He was not the kind of man who could compartmentalize. Jonny Evans was Navy. He was space. He was a fine-honed instrument of man at his scientific best. He had never rejected her — just gently put her aside. And she had understood. This had always been the nature of the man. One thing at a time. One job. Do *that* job.

But as of the moment they had let him and the others out of quarantine and he had returned home — through the round of banquets, through the noisy, insane maze of personal appearances — meetings with heads of state — the trip to Moscow — the whole unbelievable crowded calendar of the Most Important Man on Earth, she had sensed something ... something. The dreams weren't it. The dreams were a manifestation of whatever it was. And whatever it was loomed giant and yet formless in their bed at night — a barrier between the man and woman.

He rose from the bed and walked back over to the dresser to butt his cigarette out in an ashtray.

Monica felt concerned. But he felt something else again. Was it fear? He had never felt afraid. Screaming down on a MIG over Seoul — there had never been fear. Sitting in the command module at the Cape and feeling the thunderous power of the surge skyward — that had not come with fear either. The descent toward the moon, actively conscious of the hundreds of malfunctions that could have swallowed them up at the moment — this had not frightened him. But as he stood there, looking into his dark faceless reflection, he knew that he had brought back something other than rock samples from that distant barren body. He carried that something with him day and night. It began to show itself in his dreams, but upon awakening — it scurried away to hide behind the wall of his unconscious. And God, he wanted to know what it was.

He butted out the cigarette, peered at the luminous dial of his wristwatch, which he never took off, then smiled across at his wife. "3:30," he said. "I think it's getting light out."

"Moon Man," Monica said, "come back down to earth and get back to bed."

She held out her arms to him. He climbed in beside her and held her very close. He felt the soft long length of her and smelled the woman sweetness of her, but even at that moment the "something" stuck its grotesque head around the corner of his consciousness and made him sweat.

"Grimsby."

She felt his body grow taut. "What, Jonny?" she whispered. "What is it?"

He shook his head. "Nothing," he answered. "Nothing. Just that ... just that damned name — Grimsby!"

"Does the name Grimsby do anything to you?" Colonel Appleby tacked it on as the twenty-fifth question, deliberately trying to sandwich it in, so that it would not appear to be especially weighted. But Evans, sitting in front of him, understood. He lit a cigarette and then looked across at the doctor. "Is it supposed to?" he asked.

Appleby looked down at the pile of papers on his desk. "You brought the name back with you."

"My wife's gotten to you," Evans said.

Appleby looked up. "Gotten to me?" He shook his head. "Nobody 'got to me,' Commander. This isn't a conspiracy."

"What is it?" Evans' voice was blunt.

Colonel Appleby looked down at the file again. "Hopefully, it's an unpeeling of the layers of your unconscious." He looked up and grinned. "We're kind of in the same boat, Commander. You're pioneering on the moon. And some of us down here are pioneering in a most inexact science called 'Space Medicine.' You worry about orbiting — we worry about prolonged weightlessness, atmospheric pressure, radiation, body heat, increased gravity or decreased gravity, and a couple of dozen other items that we're still groping around with."

Evans leaned back in his chair. "Not the least of which is psychiatry," he said.

Appleby studied him. "If this will put you any more at ease, Commander, nobody thinks you're a candidate for analysis. Far from it."

"Then why the questions?" Evans asked.

"Then why the constant repetition of the obscure name?" Appleby asked.

Evans reached across to butt his cigarette out in the ashtray on Appleby's desk. "It's just a ... a name."

"A name you repeat in your sleep."

"I could be dredging it up from twenty ... thirty years ago."

Appleby nodded. "Altogether possible … decidedly probable." He half-turned in his chair to look out the window — the long line of launching pads stretched out across the sand. "But let me ask you this, Commander. The name is of sufficient import for you to hang on to it and research it. Why?"

Evans started. "What do you mean, 'research it'?"

"You've been trying to track it down," Appleby said, "in a couple of libraries."

"My wife again," Evans said.

Appleby shrugged. "What the hell difference does it make? So your wife told me. Now *you* tell me. What did you find out in the library?"

Evans' voice became more hesitant. "I … I checked out the name. I wondered if … if I'd come across it somewhere. In school maybe."

"Did you?"

Evans shook his head. "I found three Grimsbys in the encyclopedia. 'John J. Grimsby. Oil painter. 1838.' 'Walter Grimsby. Educator — South Carolina. 1840's'. And a 'Franklin Grimsby. Union Army Officer. Under Lincoln. Expert on Fortifications.' "

"Ever run across them before?"

"Not that I know of."

"But the name persists."

Evans nodded. "The name persists."

Appleby lit his pipe; then he looked down at the file. "You want to go on with this?" He raised his eyes to Evans' face. "I mean, do you want to come in here periodically and … and talk about it?"

Evans took out the pack of cigarettes again. "Talk about what?" he asked. "Hell, I'm ready to let loose of it right now."

"Fine," Appleby said. "I'm ready to let you. With this proviso. If you *don't* let loose of it — I *want* you to come in here and continue to talk about it. I'll tell you something, Commander. You let a little item like this take hold — it can grow into a big item, and it can raise hell with you."

"Fixation." The single word was a question.

Appleby nodded. "It works that way sometimes. Small, insignificant little aberration. You don't check it, it starts to take over."

Evans slowly rose from the chair, looking down at the unlit cigarette in his hand. "I can't figure it out. I'd let loose of it right now, except —"

"Except?"

Evans looked at him. "Except that I relate it to ... to Apollo. It has something to do with being on the moon." He shook his head. "But I can't get a fix on it."

"In the dream," Appleby said, "you're carrying a plaque. You start to put it down. Is that when the name comes up?"

Evans started to perspire. "I don't know. I start to put the plaque down, and then I draw a blank on it. I don't remember what happened then. I remember walking back to the module. I remember everything else about the mission. But there's a period of ... oh ... maybe just a minute. That's what I draw a blank on. But I'm not conscious of the name Grimsby coming in then. It's just that ... there's that ... there's that blackout period."

Appleby closed the folder and looked at his watch. "I think that ought to do it for today, Commander. This is Thursday. Come on back on Monday if that's convenient." He looked up. "Free on Monday?"

"I'm supposed to be in Washington Sunday night. President's Scientific Council is having a three-day meeting. The whole Apollo crew is supposed to be there."

Appleby sucked on his pipe. "What's it like?" he asked. "The celebrity thing. Please you, does it?"

Evans shrugged. "Sometimes not so bad. Sometimes a pain in the rump."

Appleby nodded. "I've no doubt," he said. "The price of fame."

"I was the first."

Appleby looked up sharply. Evans had just suddenly blurted it out. And at the moment he looked confused. "I'm sorry," Appleby said, his eyes suddenly clinical. "What did you say?"

Evans shook his head. "Nothing."

"You were the 'first' — isn't that what you said?"

Evans wet his lips. "I ... I guess I said that."

"Why?"

" 'Why' what?"

"Why did you say that just then?" asked Appleby.

Evans looked unnerved for the first time. "I ... I wasn't actually conscious of saying it. I guess it was just a ... just an instinctive thing."

Appleby was like a hound dog on a scent. "Kind of odd, though, isn't it? I mean — suddenly you come out with a statement like that." There was a silence; then Appleby pointed to the chair. "Why don't you sit down for a couple of more minutes? Let's talk about that last thing."

Evans slowly sank back into the chair, looking off in another direction. "I say that in my sleep, too. My wife says I ... I end the dream that way."

Appleby nodded, his face very serious. He tapped the folder. "I have that in here. I'm wondering if it relates."

Evans looked at him questioningly.

"The name Grimsby ... and that thing you just said. About being 'the first.' " He opened up the folder again, turned a couple of pages, his finger darting around the typewritten lines, then stopped and poked at one of them. " 'The first. I'm the first. Nobody before me. Nobody ahead of me. I'm the first.' " He looked up from the folder. "That's what you say in your dream." There was another silence. "That's important to you, isn't it, Evans?"

"What?"

"Being first. Being first at anything."

"You tell me." It wasn't defiance. It was just that he could no longer fence with the man. And he suddenly felt very tired.

"You were the first kid in your high school," Appleby said, "to run a four-and-a-half-minute mile. You were the first in your town to get an Annapolis appointment. You were the first in your Annapolis class to get your wings. And you were the first in your group to apply for astronauts. See a pattern there?"

Evans tried to smile. "Aggressive bastard, I guess."

Appleby looked down at the file again. "It *is* a pattern. And you were the first man to land on the moon." He looked up. "Let's talk about *that*."

Once again Evans rose from the chair. "Colonel," he said very evenly, "there are two hundred astronauts who would've cut off an arm to be the first. Now, *that's* not an aberration. That's a character trait peculiar to astronauts. That's why we joined the program. Or, at least, it's one of the reasons."

Appleby nodded. "I'll buy that," he said. "But in your case —"

"In my case, what?"

"In your case — it suggests something a little bit more than an ambition. It suggests, perhaps ... a preoccupation. A kind of ... a kind of desperation."

Evans turned and started toward the door.

"Coming back Monday?"

Evans turned to him. "I don't think so."

"Whatever you say," Appleby said. "But I'll be here."

"At the risk of sounding a little paranoiac," Evans said, "I'd appreciate it if you wouldn't keep this backyard line open to my wife. If she's got any concerns about me ... or if *you* do ... why don't we just make it a threesome?"

Appleby rose from behind the desk. "You want everything out in the open — right?"

"That'll be S.O.P. from now on," Evans said.

Appleby nodded. "That's the way it *shall* be." He pointed a pencil toward Evans. "But now hear this, Commander. I'm the project medicine man. Your job is to walk on the moon. Mine is to observe how you walk when you come back. Said observation will continue."

"A little after the fact, isn't it?"

Appleby shook his head. "After *your* fact, maybe — but there'll be several hundred more of you blasting off from here over the years. We're going to want to know what happns to that Inner Ear, the Respiratory System, the Arteries — *and the Mind!*"

"The mind?" Evans nearly shouted it.

Grimsby.

"The mind, Commander."

Grimsby.

"Well, you can sure as hell bring a notary in here right now, Colonel — and I'll get this down on paper that there's not one Goddamned thing wrong with my mind."

Grimsby.

"Now you're acting paranoiac," Appleby said.

Grimsby.

"I'm being treated like one."

Grimsby.

"Not at all. Nobody brought up the subject of paranoia except you, yourself."

Evans stood at the door, conscious of an unreasonable hostility. He forced his voice down an octave. "I'm not sure when I'll be back from Washington. There's a banquet Sunday night. There's another press conference Monday morning."

"Just let me know," Appleby said softly. "I'll be here. And I'll be here on Tuesday and also on Wednesday. Thursday, I like to play golf. But that can wait until Friday. In short, why don't you just come back whenever the spirit moves?"

Evans went out the door, saying nothing further. He felt shaken for some reason — and insecure. And the most foreign of all emotions — panic — followed him down the corridor and out into the sunny afternoon. He paused by a wire mesh fence to stare out at one of the launching pads.

Grimsby.

I'll be a son of a bitch, he thought. To get so ... so hung up by an obscure name. Stupid and meaningless and unrelated. And so totally pointless. Just a name.

But down deep, he knew. The ordered, logical, reasoned pattern of his thinking was altogether explicit on this point. It wasn't just a name. The name was the symptom. The sickness ... the compulsion, or whatever it was — that was the hang-up.

He walked across the graveled parking lot to his car. He got in and started the engine, then turned on the radio. Loud. Rock 'n' roll. He left it on as he pulled out of the parking lot. Let it drown out the name. Let the Mamas and the Papas twang out a pattern of noise to occupy his mind.

Good-bye, Grimsby — wherever you are. I hearby drum you out of my psyche. I cashier you out of my thought patterns. That frigging, intrusive little gremlin — I take leave of you.

He drove down the Coast Highway toward his home. He looked at the line of launching pads and the skeletal structures of the space ventures still on the boards. And the music stayed on, loud and persistent. But alongside of him, in the passenger seat — perched there, omniscient and lasting — was Grimsby. And by the time he pulled his car into the driveway, Lt. Commander Evans could barely control the shaking of his hands, and he felt sobs of panic rising up in his chest like nausea.

He entered the house and went directly upstairs to the bedroom, closing the door behind him.

Monica, down below in the kitchen, heard his footsteps entering and then the bedroom door closing. She listened then to the silence and finally walked over to the telephone and dialed a number. She asked for Colonel Appleby at the base.

"Colonel Appleby," she said when she heard his voice at the other end, "this is Monica Evans. What ... what happened? What do you think?"

Appleby, on the other end, said, "I can't tell you *what* happened, Mrs. Evans. I can only tell you that *something* happened — and I have a feeling it may take us awhile to find out what it was."

He sat stiffly in his dress-whites at the speaker's table, flanked by the other astronauts. A scientist was at the rostrum — a German — his voice a droning Prussian beehive of scientific jargon. And as he sat there, Evans thought about paranoia. Had Charlie Willmers, his partner in Falcon, looked at him oddly? Had Jimmy Webster, the command-module pilot, pounded him on the back too forcefully — and wasn't that smile painted on? And hadn't they been looking at him all evening out of the sides of their eyes?

He took a sip of the lukewarm coffee in front of him and thought to himself that he'd sure as hell better snap out of it. Such was the stuff of one helluva neurosis. "Good morning, Commander" — and what the hell did they mean by that? He shook his head and put the coffee cup down and tried to take a fix on the ponderous broken-English address of the scientist. A few of the words filtered in.

"Zo you zee zat we owe a tremendous debt of gratitude to zose space pioneers who in makeshift laboratories, und with primitive tools, established zee fundamental principles that unlocked zee doors to our own exploration of space —"

The droning voice went on. Willmers leaned over to him and whispered, "How the hell long does this last?"

Evans formed a smile in return and shook his head, then checked his watch, looked out over the banquet hall, aware of eyes returning his look — the congressmen and their wives; scientists; a sprinkling of military personnel. The Vice-President sat at an oval table in the corner, whispering something to a cabinet member, whose wife was sound asleep at his elbow. The affair had gone on too long. The room was much too hot. The enthusiasm had sneaked out after the third address of the evening. And the little German, currently occupying the front of the microphones, had a voice like Miltown.

"To zee Chinese we owe much. Und in zee middle of zee thirteenth century, zee name Marcus Graecus comes to mind; he made an extract from zee works of Albertus Magnus, und zee 'English power-monk,' Roger Bacon — zis work appeared in zee Greek language, but it is now available only in zee Latin translation under zee subtitle 'Lieber Ignium Ad Zomburendum Hostes' und zere are ozzer names zat come to mind. Sir William Congreve. William Hale. Dr. Robert Goddard. C. N. Hickman —"

Evans rubbed his eyes, battling against fatigue and boredom. The coffee cup was empty, and he turned to see if any water were still on the platform.

The Vice-President chuckled audibly from his table.

And at the podium, the German scientist continued his monotone acknowledgment of space pioneers. "We must, uff course, never forget zee debt owed to Sir Isaac Newton. To every action on any object, zere is und equal opposite reaction on zum ozzer object. Thus, if 'M' is zee mass of a rocket und 'V' is zee velocity und if 'M' is zee mass of zee propellent und 'V' is zee velocity, zen it can be shown zat 'V' equals V LOGe. Now zis latter equation is reasonably accurate for rockets where 'M' is not more zan fifty percent of 'M.' I refer to large 'M' und small 'm,' und uff course — we cannot forget zose obscure und little-heralded pioneers of space like ... Franklin Grimsby."

A fly buzzed around the empty coffee cup in front of the Vice-President.

A waiter rattled a tray of dishes on his way back into the kitchen.

The wife of the cabinet member dozed on.

Lt. Commander Evans rose to his feet, his skin clammy, his heart suddenly smashing against his rib cage.

Grimsby. Franklin Grimsby.

The little German scientist suddenly looked up over his steel-rimmed glasses. "Just zink of zee incredible vision of men like Grimsby. Now zis dates back to zee middle of zee nineteenth century when zee principles of rocket propulsion had hardly even been touched. Und yet ... here was zis altogether obscure engineer who —"

"No!"

The audience looked up, staring at Evans. He had pounded his fist on the table, smashing it against the coffee cup. He stood there, swaying left and right, his eyes fever-bright in a chalk face.

"No, Goddamn it," he screamed, "*I* was the first. I swear to God — *I* was the first!"

The nightmare run across the room, past the staring, bewildered faces — smashing against a waiter at the door, tripping over the foot of a senator as he was reentering the room. And then out in the street — a hot, muggy Washington night — heavy air descending in wet waves — and Evans ran. He ran past the giant Lincoln sitting serenely on his chair and past the partly lit stiletto of the Washington Monument and past the stately pillared tribute to Jefferson. And still he ran. He hit a lamppost with stunning, bone-breaking force and found himself on his face on concrete.

And then he was back on the moon. The concrete had turned into fine-grained ash. It was the black night of the moon. In his hand he carried the plaque. He cradled it like Moses. And he looked down at the spot where it was to go.

And then he saw it.

A piece of rock with the deeply embedded scrawl made by some metal tool, half-buried in the ground — weathered and pitted and aged. But it could be read.

"To That Generation of Man Who Will Follow Me Here. Welcome To The Moon On This 11th Day of July, 1865. I, Franklin Grimsby, Major, Army of the Republic, set foot on this barren place. I claim it for the United States of America at the behest of Abraham Lincoln, President of the United States."

Two lines had been worn smooth and obliterated. And then another line close to the sand could be partially read.

"... And since it is impossible to bring a message of our success back to Earth, I ask that whoever follows us here — at whatever time — bring back the message of our success to the people of a —"

The rest of the rock was buried in the sand, but already Commander Evans' heavily encased space boot had begun to destroy it. He kicked at it three times, splitting the rock; then he stomped on it until it began to dissolve like a mummified piece of parchment. And when he was finished, nothing was left. Just little clumps of rock. And nothing more.

They found him lying on the sidewalk, body stiff, eyes fixed and open, fingernails embedded in his palms and drawing blood.

In his office a week later, Colonel Appleby read the letter for the dozenth time. It was from Professor Hans Wuer, the eminent German rocket expert who made occasional speeches in Washington, D.C. Appleby looked down at the last paragraph.

"... so I can assure you, Colonel Appleby, I am at a loss to understand the reaction of Lt. Commander Evans. In my research, the name 'Franklin Grimsby' has come up only sporadically, and usually very briefly. As I indicated to you on the phone, he is an altogether obscure, mid-nineteenth century engineer who believed that by the use of a highly concentrated gun powder, primed and exploded in stages, a vehicle could be blasted out of the earth's gravitational pull. There is no record that he ever advanced beyond a rather primitive hypothesis —"

Appleby put the letter down and looked at his watch. He was due at the Bethesda Naval Hospital that afternoon — a sixth visit to a patient named Evans, lying in a catatonic state in isolation. He folded the letter up and inserted it into the Evans file, put it back into his desk, and locked the drawer.

There were two other letters lost to sight and memory that still existed on the planet Earth. One was in a dusty trunk in the attic of a dairy farmer named Grimsby, just outside of Madison, Wisconsin.

It read, in part: "... so you see, Major Grimsby, I cannot reemphasize enough the desperate need for secrecy in this venture. Neither the Congress nor the people would be sympathetic to such an expenditure of funds for a scientific project whose success or failure would never be known to them. The moneys allocated to you will come from a special fund. I have only this further to say to you: In the past year I have witnessed perhaps the best of man's courage. But your proposed voyage into the sky suggests a courage that is beyond language. You tell me that you hope to commence the building of the vehicle now and that the journey would begin sometime in April of next year. I can assure you of this. When our victory in this desperate war is completed, I shall make a public pronouncement that Major Franklin Grimsby has taken a giant step in the service of mankind. A. Lincoln. February, 1864."

The other letter was wedged into a crack inside a Chippendale desk in the basement of the White House. It read, in part: "... so you see, Mr. President, even if I should land on the moon, there will be no way for this success to be made known. It is a one-way trip. But someday other men will make this journey and know whether or not I *was* a success. Your interest and good wishes and your unquestioning support makes me proud, indeed. Your obedient servant, Franklin Grimsby. Major. Army of the Republic."

In the small cubicle of a room in the Bethesda Naval Hospital, Lt. Commander Jonathan Cornelius Evans looked up at the ceiling. He saw neither the nurse nor Colonel Appleby nor the stricken, pinched white features of his wife hovering over him. Every now and then his teeth would clench.

"I was the first," he murmured. "I swear to God — I was the first. In the whole history of man ... nobody was ahead of me."

Then the glazed, empty eyes traversed the room. That little wraith of truth buried so deep, chained and broken-winged, fluttered briefly to the surface.

"Does the name Grimsby do anything to you?" his voice asked, as if in a tomb. "Does it? Does it mean anything to you? Grimsby?"

And at the Cape, Apollo II stood straight and tall in its launching pad — an eager cylinder waiting to cut its bonds — waiting to carry yet a third man for a walk on the moon.

CLEAN KILLS AND OTHER TROPHIES

"After dinner," Colonel Dittman said to his son, sitting at the far end of the long, thirty-foot oaken table, "we'll show Mr. Pierce my Hunting Room."

Dittman, Jr., pale, silent, simply nodded.

Pierce, sitting halfway between the two, called on his poor stretched tired mouth to smile once again, as he'd been smiling all through the painful evening. The venison, tough, gamy, stringy, sat heavy inside of him, shoveled down with effort. The wine was a flinty Moselle — tart and too warm, but he'd had five glasses of it and he felt his eyes heavy-lidded, his attention wandering out of sight. He looked from his host to his host's son and wondered vaguely about the genetic vagaries that produced offspring so different from their fathers.

Colonel Archie Dittman sat there at the head of the table, lean and erect, white hair cropped over a long-jawed patrician face. He wore a smoking jacket, baroque, but perfectly tailored. Throughout the two-hour dinner he had kept the conversation moving — directing it like traffic — short sporadic thrusts into conversational areas, jabbed at, then left behind. Taxes. (They were confiscatory.) Campus dissent. (Kick those spoiled, self-indulgent weirdos in the ass and draft them.) Race relations. (The mistake had not been slavery — the black bastards shouldn't have been brought over here in the first place.) And through it all Pierce had sat there with a fixed, strained smile — as befitting the youngest member of a law firm that handled Colonel Dittman's legal affairs at fifty thousand dollars a year retainer. Pierce then turned to look in the opposite direction at the son. Dittman, Jr., had his father's lankiness, but there was no other resemblance. That he deferred to the father was altogether obvious. Only when the older Dittman used the word "nigger" did Dittman, Jr., seem to flinch perceptively, but he had not uttered a word during the entire meal. Earlier, Pierce had tried to draw him out, asking him about his graduation from college that spring, his plans, his interests. The pale, washed-out blue eyes simply fixed on Pierce — the broad but bony shoulders shrugging as if to say to Pierce that any and all decisions came from the other end of the table. Dittman, Sr., verified this. What was his son planning to do? They would think about this. What was his interest? He, Dittman, Sr., was currently taking that under advisement. How had he liked college? Colonel Dittman had allowed that college nowadays was obviously a monumental waste of time.

"Your average university nowadays, Mr. Pierce," Colonel Dittman had said, "produces a somewhat formless mass of jellied consommé; a generation of social workers, better equipped to play a tambourine at a Salvation Army soup kitchen than to roll up their sleeves and do an honest-to-God day's work, turning an honest profit."

Dittman had glared across the table at his son — not just in anger, Pierce noted, but with naked dislike that was beginning to turn a painful evening into an unbearable one. But the boy had not responded. Those pale, spiritless blue eyes looked downward to his plate like flags dipped in surrender. And the Colonel had looked across at Pierce with a thin, hating little smile as if to say, "And there, Mr. Pierce, you observe the scion of the family — that silent, cheek-turning embarrassment sitting at the opposite end of the table."

All three had a brandy glass in their hands as Dittman led the way into the Hunting Room.

Out of Metro-Goldwyn-Mayer, Culver City, California, Pierce thought as they entered the vast, paneled mausoleum with the high cathedraled ceiling. Thirty-foot oak beams butterflied up to a point almost two stories high. There was a sunken fireplace with a mantel ten feet off the ground. The roaring fire was an animated cartoon, too big and too hot to be real. Above, and surrounding it, were two rows of sawed-off animal heads ornately mounted on polished plaques, each with its own glass-eyed resignation to both violent death and permanent exhibition. On the opposite side of the room were perhaps twenty glass cabinets housing rifles and pistols of every description. But if any man had a special milieu — a private province of his own — this room bore the imprimatur of Colonel Archie Dittman. He seemed to blend with it as he entered the room. Standing underneath the mounted head of a lion, it was as if he were posing right after the hunt, and the truncated beast over his head had been ordained to spend his eternity on that very wall.

Pierce's father had told him about the room and had tried to brief him on Dittman.

"An oddball, Bill," his father had said. "Sinew that walks like a man. Willful, cruel — a suit of armor come to life long after his time." That had been his father's description. But somewhat apologetically he had added, "But the son of a bitch pays a lot of salaries around here, and with the son coming of age, you're going to have to sit down with that miserable old fart of a tyrant and discuss the trust with him. He'll no doubt ask you for the weekend. He used to ask me when his wife was alive."

Pierce recalled the conversation. Standing there in the overheated room with his stomach sending up nauseous little waves of protest, he made a mental note that on Monday he would tell his father that no amount of retainer would ever allow him to be a weekend guest again of a nineteenth-century land baron who obviously spent his days killing animals and his nights emasculating his son.

Pierce looked across at the son, who had sat quietly down in a chair several feet from the fireplace.

Dittman, Jr., sipped briefly at his brandy, then put the glass down. He stared into the fire. The flames formed illuminated patterns on his face.

Pierce was at that moment struck by the pain that showed on that face. Not just discomfort. Pain. To be a weekend guest of Colonel Archie Dittman was a prolonged discomfort. To be his son — this had to be a special kind of agony.

"How is your father, Mr. Pierce?" Colonel Dittman asked.

"Still very active," Pierce answered.

"I've no doubt. And an altogether competent lawyer."

There was a silence as Dittman inventoried Pierce. "Are you as good as he is?"

A slightly deeper hue of color appeared on Pierce's face. Embarrassment added to the wine and brandy. "Probably not," he admitted. "My father handles pretty much everything. But mostly trial stuff. My work is limited to trusts." As he said this, he had a secret hope that this might remind Dittman of the purpose of his visit. Archie, Jr., would be twenty-one on the first of the following month. Something in the neighborhood of two and a half million dollars' worth of stocks and bonds would revert to the boy as of that date. But Dittman had turned his back and was walking the length of one of the walls. Pierce felt the urgent need to sit down. The nausea had become a burning thing inside, and he was beginning to feel sick.

Dittman stopped underneath the head of a horned animal. He pointed to it. "Know anything about guns, Pierce, or hunting?"

"I'm afraid not." Pierce looked up and down the walls. "I take it that's your hobby."

Dittman smiled. "My ... my hobby?" He emphasized the word "hobby" as if it were some kind of an effete variation on croquet played on girls' schools' lawns. "It's hardly a hobby," he said. "It's what I do with my life." He reached up to tap the plaque underneath the animal. "I don't think there's any game on earth I haven't stalked," he said. "Stalked and killed. The baby above me is a thomson's gazelle. I got that in the Nyeri Forest. The horns are sixteen and three-quarter inches long. It's mentioned in *Ward's Records of Big Game.*"

Pierce nodded politely, then looked past the unfortunate gazelle to the big lion's head alongside.

Dittman noted the look. "Like that one?" he asked.

Pierce nodded and thought about how one responded to a question like that. Could someone "like" the remnants of a dead animal? Would you express admiration, or just how the hell would one make comment on the trophies of a kill?

Dittman did not allow him to ponder the etiquette of the situation. He moved a few steps over to stand underneath the lion.

"I'll tell you about this son of a bitch," he said, pointing to it. "He gave me trouble. He gave me all kinds of trouble."

Pierce looked at the slit glass eyes. Even counterfeit and manufactured, they still looked fierce and enraged.

"I got him on a rainy day," Dittman said, sipping on his brandy. "Lions are temperamental beasts — subject to moods. Rainy weather makes them nervous. And darkness stimulates them." He nodded toward the lion's head again. "They hunt at night. And I hunted *him* at night."

Pierce nodded politely, not really giving a good Goddamn what affected lions or when they hunted, or anything else about them. He was sleepy, bored, ill at ease. Dittman, Jr., he observed, was still sitting silently in the chair across from the fireplace.

"The other problem," Dittman continued, "is that they can see in the dark." He reached up to touch the lion's mane. It was a flowing crown around the head, like a growing thing. "So for openers, my friend here had all the advantage. Night. Rain. And a sense of smell that is damned uncanny."

Pierce found himself staring at those glass eyes and wondering about what advantage an animal *ever* had when men with guns dedicated themselves to destroying it.

"I had my gun boy throw stones at it," Dittman said. "Then I shouted at it, and it charged me. He was about fifty yards away when he started the charge. Ever see a lion charge, Mr. Pierce?"

Pierce shook his head. The closest he'd ever been to a lion was to look at one through a cage at the San Diego Zoo when he was twelve years old.

"They get up to about forty miles an hour. And, by God, you've only got one chance to do the job. This son of a bitch weighed close to five hundred pounds. Goddamned express train. If you don't stop him before he reaches you — you can forget about hunting and everything else."

Pierce nodded. He wanted to look at his watch. The heavy, uncomfortable feeling of too much food and too much drink, and there was that nausea again. He put down his brandy glass. The brandy was getting to him too. He was beginning to feel a little disoriented. Was he being too quiet and too unresponsive? It came to him that perhaps the next comment should be his. He blinked his eyes, forcing them to look at least somewhat interested.

"He's ... he's beautiful," Pierce said, nodding toward the lion.

Colonel Dittman's smile was a little slit of condescension. "Beautiful," he repeated, as if hearing a foreign word. "Beautiful. I guess you could call him beautiful — if a killer can be beautiful. And they're killers, all right, Mr. Pierce. I've seen them stampede a herd of cattle and kill them off one by one in less than five minutes. Do you remember that time, Arch?" For the first time he had directed a question at his son — a belated acknowledgment that he was even in the room.

Young Dittman nodded but continued to stare across at the fire.

Pierce felt light-headed. By God, he thought, I'm getting drunk. I'm actually getting drunk. He picked up his brandy glass and took another sip. "Do they hunt in groups?" he asked. He had decided at that moment that he would let Dittman broach the legal question of the trust. For the time being, he'd simply play the interested guest until such time as this Great White Hunter would run out of his favorite topic. Dittman obviously relished talk of the hunt, but if he received no animated response — how long could the monologue go? Pierce decided that he'd give the old boy a few more minutes to wallow around in his favorite subject.

"A family of lions is called a pride," Dittman explained. "I've seen as many as eighteen or twenty — from the grand old male down to the newborn cubs." He left the lion and sauntered down the line of animal heads. "Zebra, Cape buffalo — and this big black hairy bastard is a gorilla. Illegal, but damned good sport. And his cousin alongside is a baboon. Not many people understand baboons."

Pierce finished the brandy and heard himself chuckle, and he really didn't give a damn. As a matter of fact, he didn't give a damn about the trust fund either, or the silent boy in the chair, or this ramrod host of his — Archie Dittman, Sr. Hunter by avocation. Rich man by inheritance. Colonel by honorary investiture. Then, a quick look across at the son — that silent, defeated next-in-the-Dittman-line. "I don't know too many baboons," he said idiotically. Then he laughed aloud, at the same time finishing what little brandy there was left in his glass.

Just a shade of displeasure crossed the Colonel's face. "They're brave," he said, "and they're intelligent. They're also cruel as hell. I've seen them catch native chickens and amuse themselves by plucking the birds alive just to watch them scream and struggle." He shook his head. "I don't think there are many things as cruel as a jungle animal."

It was the brandy, Pierce decided, that made him feel so suddenly hostile toward Dittman. And it was the brandy, he was quite sure of this, that forced him to speak out at that moment. "Man isn't exactly a humanitarian, Colonel."

Dittman smiled. "Man?" he asked. "You think man is more cruel than the animal?"

It was more than hostility now. Pierce despised the hell out of Dittman. "Man *is* an animal, isn't he?" he said. "And he's the only animal who kills for the pleasure and the sport of it."

Dittman smiled. The thin-lipped mouth. The slit. He looked across at his son. "Sounds like you, Archie. Sounds exactly like you." Then he turned toward Pierce. "Junior over there doesn't much care for hunting either." He moved across the room closer to Pierce. "There's a tribe in Africa, Mr. Pierce, called the Masai. Every now and then they pick out the least active of their senior citizens and put them out into the bush for the hyenas to eat alive." Again the thin smile. "Didn't Adam Smith have a theory about overpopulation?" Then, without waiting for a reply — "Well, those painted niggers didn't require fancy economists to tell them how to keep the population down. They acted out of instinct. Survival instinct."

The ice-blue eyes bored into Pierce. "Now, you'd call that cruel, wouldn't you, Mr. Pierce?" he asked. "My son feels that it's cruel."

Pierce looked briefly at the boy, then back to the father. "I'd call it savage," he said. "Uncivilized. But that's death with a purpose at least — as horrible as it is."

"And killing animals," Dittman continued on, leading Pierce along like a professor, "is heartless and uncompassionate. That your point, Mr. Pierce?"

Pierce this time deliberately looked at his watch. The nausea rose dangerously up into his throat. He was not too far away from bolting out of the room. He took a deep breath. "I really don't know very much about it, Colonel," he said, "but it's getting late. I think the three of us have something to discuss here." He nodded toward the boy, bringing him back into the fold.

But already Dittman had turned his back and was walking across the room over to the gun cases. "I don't suppose you know anything about guns either, do you, Mr. Pierce?" he asked.

Pierce felt perspiration on his forehead, and the cold clammy feeling of the preliminary stages of tomorrow's hangover. "No, Colonel," he said, "I don't know very much about guns either."

"I've got some dandies over here," Dittman said proudly.

Pierce swallowed. He felt his protesting stomach wanting to send back the gift of venison and wine through the orifice where it had first been introduced. "I'm afraid, Colonel," he said, "that I'm … I'm a little tired." He looked around, forgetting at the moment where he'd left his briefcase. Then he remembered it was in the front hall. "I have the papers in my briefcase, Colonel. It's not really complicated. Just the instructions to the stock-transfer agent to arrange the distribution of the stock to the beneficiary." Again he nodded toward Dittman, Jr.

Colonel Dittman was in the process of opening the first of the glass cases. It was as if Pierce had never even said anything about the trust. "This is an interesting weapon here," he said, taking out a small carbine. "It's a Sharps breechloading percussion carbine used by the Union Army in the Civil War." He tapped with a forefinger on the case. "Alongside of it in there is a Harpers Ferry flint pistol marked with an American eagle. You can see the words 'Harpers Ferry, U.S.' on the handle."

He replaced the carbine and closed the glass case, then started up the line to the next one.

"Colonel —" Pierce was beginning to feel desperate. "If we could just talk about the trust. Now, your signature will be required —"

Dittman had already opened the next glass case. "Over here," he said, "is a revolving flintlock pistol by Elisha Haydon Collier of Boston. The machine work was by Henry Nock. This has got to be worth at least five thousand dollars." He reached in and took out another pistol. "This," he said, "is a .54 C.B. Allen-Elgin Cutlass Pistol made in 1837. It's a combination gun with an attached blade." He tapped on the glass case with the butt end of the pistol. "In there," he said, "is a Colt .44 percussion dragoon revolver."

"Colonel," Pierce said with as much force as he could conjure up.

Dittman turned and looked across the room at him; then he very slowly, deliberately, methodically replaced the weapon, closed the glass case, and took out a cigar as he retraced his steps across the room to stand very close to Pierce. "You were saying, Mr. Pierce? Something about the trust?"

Pierce nodded. "I'll get my briefcase, and —"

"There'll be no need to get your briefcase, Mr. Pierce. I know precisely the extent of the securities in the trust. I know the amounts, the names. I know the current values. I can even give you the certificate numbers."

He took out a gold lighter, lit the cigar, took a long, luxurious drag, then ambled very slowly over to a chair near where his son sat, and sat down. "I want to add a codicil to the disposition of the contents of the trust."

"A codicil?" Pierce asked, blinking.

"That's right," Dittman responded evenly. "Something in the nature of a proviso."

"Like what?" Pierce asked.

Dittman leaned forward in the chair. "The reversion of the trust," he said, "takes place in exactly fifteen days. If, during those fifteen days, my son has not killed himself an animal, I want the trust dissolved."

Archie, Jr., stared at the fire. It was as if he felt himself invisible or alone in the room. A birthright was being stripped from him like an animal pelt. But the pale, taut face showed not a flicker of reaction.

Pierce kept staring at Dittman. Perhaps, he thought, this was the older man's humor. Maybe he was being funny now. He tried to smile. "That trust," he started to explain, "is irrevocable, Colonel. You can't change it."

"Can't I?" Dittman's voice sounded light, almost playful.

"No, sir. You can't change it in any way."

"No way at all, huh?"

Pierce tried to smile. "Only if the boy were ... were proven incompetent." He let his smile move over to Archie, Jr., like headlights on a turning car.

Archie Dittman, for the first time, turned to look at his father.

"What about it, Archie?" the Colonel said. "You've got a couple of million dollars' worth of gilt-edged stocks and bonds waiting for you. You're aware of that, aren't you?"

Archie, Jr. nooded. His voice was so soft that Pierce had to lean forward to catch it.

"I'm quite aware of it," the boy said.

"He's quite aware of it," the Colonel repeated, as if translating for the lawyer. "He's quite aware of the fact that he'll be a millionaire." Then he turned again toward his son. "And are you also aware, Archie, that I have just tried to put some strings on the package?"

The boy nodded.

"And are you also aware of the nature of the conditions I'm trying to impose?"

"I heard what you said," Archie, Jr., responded.

"I want you to kill an animal. All by yourself. With a gun."

Pierce looked at the boy. His fists were clenched. Pierce was suddenly aware of this. The Colonel was also. He looked at the boy's hands and smiled.

"Look at him, Pierce. Look at his hands. By God, he's reacting. Somebody just shot some adrenalin into the body. We're getting a reaction. It may be only a reflexive twitch. Maybe a muscular spasm. But, by God, there *is* movement." He let out a long, thin stream of cigar smoke, then let his eyes rest on Pierce. "How old are you, Mr. Pierce? Early thirties? Somewhere around there?"

Pierce nodded.

"Not a helluva lot older than my son," Dittman said, leaning back in the chair. "Now, if your old man had done to you what I'm doing to him —" He pointed to Archie. "Arbitrarily and altogether predatorily tried to screw you out of what was yours — what would you do? How would you react?"

There was a silence in the room, broken sporadically by the sound of the occasional crack of the burning logs in the fireplace.

"The question wasn't rhetorical, Mr. Pierce. What would you do?"

"I don't suppose I'd sit still for it," Pierce answered.

"Of course not. Who *would* sit still for it? You'd either get up on your two feet and square off against your father, or you'd be on a phone calling a lawyer, or you'd raise holy hell. Now, you'd do that, wouldn't you?"

"Colonel," Pierce began.

Dittman held up his hand, with the cigar in it. "Of course you would," he interrupted. "But I'll tell you what you *wouldn't* do. You wouldn't just sit there like my son is sitting there clenching his fists. Particularly if your father had just told you to do something that went completely against your grain."

Colonel Dittman rose from his chair and moved over to the fireplace. It was like a pose, Pierce thought. For men of distinction. The thin, erect, white-haired man standing there, one hand lightly touching the mantel. The whole thing, Pierce decided at that moment, was a pose. This was just some kind of ponderous joke, an after-dinner party game that a humorless man finds festive. But Archie Jr.'s hands were shaking. Maybe he'd played this game before. Get on with it, Pierce thought. Something tense was building up in the room. Something explosive.

"My son doesn't take to killing," the Colonel said from the fireplace. "No way, no method, no victim of any kind. He is a silent minority of one. I've taken him on trips to jungles, hunting preserves, African bush — places that most boys would welcome as high adventure. But not my son. Not Archie over there. When a rifle went off, I'd find him hiding in the bushes. Or on the morning of a hunt — he'd have digestive problems — like a pregnant lady." He pointed his cigar at the boy. "He has rather that look about him, wouldn't you say, Mr. Pierce? The look of the pregnant lady? Pale, suffering, that quivering-rabbit look."

Pierce waited for the boy to say something, do something, remonstrate in some way, climb down from the whipping post, and either grab the whip or at least run away. But the boy just sat there. Pierce felt a different kind of nausea, but with it came resolve. This would have to stop right now. Retainers notwithstanding, he didn't have to be a party to this. And he wouldn't be any longer.

"Colonel," Pierce said. "None of this is my business. I'm here on a very specific item. To handle the reversion of a trust fund. That's all. That's all I'm supposed to do. As to any disagreement you may have with your son —"

Dittman interrupted him. "My disagreements with my son, Mr. Pierce, are very much your business. Because they very much relate to that trust. I have no intention of handing a gravy bowl over to a nutless, faggoty, simpering little son of a bitch who dishonors me. I have no intention whatsoever."

"I'm afraid you don't have any choice in the matter, Colonel." Pierce blurted out. He could almost visualize his father's apoplectic face. (Christ on a Cross, Bill. All you had to do was to get his Goddamned signature.) But it was too late. Pierce had taken a look at the two teams and had somehow walked over to stand alongside of Archie Dittman, Jr. Die cast. Bed made and ready to sleep in. Money paid — choice made.

"What would happen" — Dittman's voice was not particularly unfriendly — "if I simply failed to put my signature on whatever it is you've brought with you? What if I simply refused to give him a dime?"

"I'm afraid you don't have that choice," Pierce answered. "First of all, you've been paying fiduciary taxes on —"

"Oh, stop that crap, Mr. Pierce. Don't give me this fiduciary nonsense or your complicated tax language or that ponderous legal crap." He pointed to Archie, Jr. "What the hell can he do to me?"

"He can sue you."

Dittman laughed aloud for the first time. "He can *sue* me? Honest to God — that cauliflower there can honest to God get himself a battery of lawyers and sue me?" Once again he laughed and shook his head. "That Goddamn vegetable can suddenly get some guts and stand up to me?"

"That would be my advice to him, Colonel." Pierce's voice was icy.

"That would be your advice, huh? Well, I'll tell you something, Mr. Pierce. This would be *my* advice to you. Go to bed and get a good night's sleep. In the morning the three of us will go out and hunt deer. Now, if *you* suffer buck fever, you may get a little bored. That's not measles. It isn't catching. It won't affect me in the slightest. But if my son over there won't pick up a gun and bring down a deer, I'll take every piece of security in that trust fund, and by Tuesday morning I'll piss it away on every speculative high-risk wildcat venture currently available on both markets or in the back room of a bookie parlor. By Wednesday morning I can turn that two and a half million dollars into toilet paper. I'm an expert at how that's done."

Pierce just stared at him. "Would you ... would you really do that?"

"Would and will," Dittman said.

Pierce turned toward Archie, Jr. "You don't have to sit still for this," he said to the boy. "I'm a witness to it. You could start proceedings in the morning in a court of law, and I'd represent you."

Archie, Jr., rose from his chair. If anything, he looked only tired. He looked briefly at his father and then at Pierce. "I don't want that, Mr. Pierce," he said softly. "He can do anything he wants."

"You see, Mr. Pierce?" the Colonel said. "I can do anything I want. I can dress him in a nightie, rob him blind, or put a boot up his butt — and he'll turn his cheek so Goddamn fast you'll think his head was built on a swivel." He flung the cigar into the open fire, looked at it for a moment then turned back to face the other two. "I'm going to bed now," he announced. "Breakfast at seven. We'll be out on the track by a quarter to eight. There'll be a weapon for both of you." He moved over to his son, standing a hand's length away. "I'm going to tell you something now, Archie. You've never done one single thing in your whole life to please me. From cradle to college diploma. You've shamed me. You've dishonored me. You've made me wish a hundred times ... a thousand times ... that there was some kind of higher law having to do with the painless eradication of imperfect infants."

Pierce let out a gasp. Involuntary. Unconscious. But audible.

Dittman ignored him. "Or some kind of ultimate computer in a maternity ward," he continued, "which could perceive weakness in an infant and prescribe accordingly."

"Colonel —" Pierce's voice was shaky. "If you keep this up, you won't leave *me* any alternative. I'll have to place a long-distance call to my father and tell him that you're incompetent."

"Me?" Dittman's voice was ice cold. "You'd have a helluva time proving that thesis, Mr. Pierce. I'm not incompetent." He pointed to the long rows of animal heads. "I happen to be one of the most efficient, deadly hunters, stalkers, and killers of wild game as there is on the Continent."

Insane, Pierce thought. Stark, raving, staring mad. Non compos mentis. No wonder Archie, Jr., remained silent. You don't remonstrate against a madness that sees singular virtue in killing. Pierce felt sympathy for the boy. His look must have showed it, because Dittman studied him for a long moment, shaking his head back and forth.

"Mr. Pierce," Dittman said, "the elemental eludes you, doesn't it? The fact that my patron saint happens to be firearms — this is incomprehensible, isn't it?"

"It's pretty Goddamn strange," Pierce retorted. The son could walk around tiptoe and in silent agony. This wouldn't be one of his *own* requirements. "You have just finished telling me, Colonel, that unless your son shoots a deer, you'll wipe him out. You'll take what is rightfully his and flush it down a drain someplace. The most charitable surmise I can come up with, Colonel, is that you're eccentric. But in most courts of law, I think that would be pretty damned good grounds for commitment."

Colonel Dittman reached across and tapped Pierce with a forefinger. "I'll tell you now," he said, "what I've told my son on many occasions. This world — from pole to pole — is a jungle. It's inhabited by various species of beasts, and one of them happens to be man. He has only one honest-to-God function — and that is to survive. There is no morality, no law, no imposed manmade dogma that should be allowed to get in the way of that survival. That he survives is the only morality there is. To survive he must be superior. And the only way he can prove that superiority is to be able to put to death any other species that tries to share his living space."

Pierce looked at the animal heads — the lion, the baboon, the gazelle — and they looked back to him with the counterfeit fury of their glass eyes. Those poor, fur-covered, horned, growling, roaring, charging, dumb beasts! They had to go get born in Africa. The Congo. The rain forests. The jungles. They had encroached on Colonel Dittman's eminent domain, and from then on, Pierce thought, those decapitated bastards would roar and charge no more. Pierce's instincts then were to leave it at that; maybe just to walk quietly out of the room and find his bedroom and go to sleep, and then return to Boston in the morning. Then, with his father, he could draw up a court order, and this fanatic in the smoking jacket could be safely ensconced in a rubber room sufficiently far away from his mounted trophies, so that he might ultimately forget his fixation that the proof of superiority lay in cordite and trigger housings.

But it was as if Dittman anticipated the thought. "I'll leave you now," he said to Pierce. "Have a little chat with my son. It'll be like discoursing with a baby blanket, but you may be able to extract a couple of his more heartrending philosophies."

Again silence. Again the crackling logs on the fire. Archie, Jr., walked over to the fireplace and again looked into the flames. He picked up a poker and manipulated the logs, causing a new sheet of fire to rise up between them. He was conscious of Pierce staring at him, and finally turned toward him. "You weren't prepared for anything like this, were you, Mr. Pierce?"

It took a moment for Pierce to speak. "Let me put it this way," he said finally. "I don't think what's needed here is a lawyer. I think a battery of psychiatrists would have their Goddamned work cut out for them."

"That's kind of funny," Archie, Jr., said.

"What is?" Pierce asked, thinking to himself that if there was any minute fragmentary piece of humor floating around there, he'd like to throw a net on it.

"Psychiatrists. I've been to one. My senior year at school I went three times a week."

"Waste of time. Waste of money. It's your father —"

"My father doesn't believe in psychiatrists."

"I believe you. His idea of a head-shrinker is very likely a pickling process practiced by pygmies with horns through their noses. Now, look, Archie —"

Archie, Jr., put the poker back into its stand. He returned to his seat. His walk, Pierce noted, was boneless. Jointless. Six feet of ganglion and skin; taut, thin, tightly stretched skin. He stood near Pierce. His angle to the fire highlighted the side of his face. There was a thin white scar that extended from the temple to the hairline.

"Whatever else he is" — the boy's voice was soft — "he's not sick. It doesn't make any difference whether or not he believes in psychiatrists. He'll never need one."

Pierce smiled his disbelief. "But you do, huh?"

The boy didn't smile back. "Yeah, Mr. Pierce," he said, "I need one. I'm the sick one."

He looked down at the floor. He was standing on a coarse buffalo hide. Pierce hadn't even noticed it before. But it fit. Death on the walls. Instruments of death across the room, all properly tagged in their glass receptacles. And death on the floor. Every damned thing in the room related to death.

"I am sick, you know, Mr. Pierce."

"No, I don't know that at all."

"If I'm not sick, why do I just stand here and let him castrate me?"

"You won't have to let him do that for much longer. In a couple of weeks you'll be able to pack your bags and move out to the other end of the earth if you want."

Archie, Jr., made a sound like a low laugh. He sat down. "I could simplify all this if I wanted to. I could just go out with him tomorrow morning and kill the deer. That's all it would take."

"It doesn't take *that*," Pierce said. "You don't have to kill a deer, swat a fly, or step on an ant. You don't have to do *anything*. As a matter of fact, all you have to do is sign your name. And by tomorrow, at lunch-time, I can get a court order in here impounding the trust. My dad's law firm could be named trustee, or a bank —"

"He'd get back at me for that."

"How?" Pierce asked. "There isn't a damned thing he could do about it."

"You don't think so? There isn't a place on earth I could go where he wouldn't follow me. And you know something else, Mr. Pierce? He'd enjoy it. That's what he likes best — stalking. That's his pleasure. To hunt something down. You give him a gun and a scent of the victim — that's the one thing on earth that makes him happy."

Archie, Jr., reached for his brandy glass and drained its contents. "You ought to see his face when he squeezes a trigger. You ought to look at him when his bullet hits home. It's like ... like an orgasm. It's the purest passion any human being can feel." He turned to look at the flames. "And I'll tell you something else," he said. "He's the twentieth-century man. A predator. And he's right that I'm the minority. I think most human beings would love to kill if they had the chance. I think the whole bloody earth would be a hunting preserve if it could be arranged that way."

"Wrong," said Pierce, suddenly feeling argumentative. "Oh God but you're wrong." Then he stopped, shook his head, and smiled. This colloquy was almost as bizarre as the situation. There he sat arguing abstractions, as if suddenly he was the public defender of predatory man. The animal heads above him were like a jury, listening with silent intensity. "I don't think you can generalize as to man's evil, Archie. He does too much good."

Archie, Jr., smiled. "Sure he does." He held up the brandy glass, turning it around in his fingers. "He gives at the office. Small spasms of contribution." He put the glass down and rose to his feet. "What should I do tomorrow, Mr. Pierce?" he asked. "Shall I knock off a deer and make him happy? Reinstate myself into the company of men? He's really not asking a helluva lot. Just sight along a little old barrel and squeeze on a little old trigger and put a bullet into a little old deer." He turned to look at the animal heads. Their fixed glass eyes seemed to look back at him.

A convocation of victims, Pierce thought. Some mounted, and one standing — but all victims. The wild ones shot to death — the pathetic-looking one on two legs, twisted and pulled out of joint by twenty-one years of intimidation and fear.

Pierce took a deep breath. "I'm going to bed, Archie," he said. "Tomorrow morning you tell me what you want me to do." He turned toward the door.

"Mr. Pierce." Archie Jr.'s voice stopped him. "What would you do?"

Pierce looked at him, halfway to the door. "What would I do?"

Archie, Jr., nodded. "Would you kill a deer for two and a half million dollars?"

Pierce actually found himself weighing the proposition. Two and a half million dollars. Enough money to saw away the umbilical and get the hell out of there, far away from the maniac in the smoking jacket. Incredibly enough, he found himself nodding. "I suppose I would," he said. "I probably would. I'd kill his Goddamned deer, and then I'd take off."

"Would you kill a man for four million? Or two men for eight?"

Pierce frowned. "Nobody's asking you to kill a man."

Archie, Jr., smiled again. "We're talking principle now." He went on before Pierce could answer. "For me to kill an animal — is about the same thing as asking you to kill an infant. Whenever he hands me a gun, Mr. Pierce, I break out into a cold sweat. I get the shakes. I get sick to my stomach. I could tell you a hundred places where it happened. And how he reacted. Once in Nairobi he hit me with a pistol butt." He involuntarily touched the white scar on his face. "Then he left me out in the bush. One of the gun bearers brought me in. And you know what my father said when he saw me?"

Pierce just stared at him.

"He said to the gun bearer — 'This is a girl child. You had no business bringing him in.' That's what he said to the gun bearer."

"Jesus, Archie," Pierce said, "that's insane —"

"Maybe in a distinguished Massachusetts law office it's insane. Or on the Boston Common it sounds insane. But out there my father made the rules. He set the standards."

"We're not in Nairobi now," Pierce said. "We're a lot closer to that law office than we are the African bush." He went over to the big double doors and opened them. "I'll see you tomorrow, Archie. We'll get this thing settled." He turned and tried to smile at the boy.

Archie, Jr., stood by the fire, running a fingertip across the scar. "I've decided," he said. "I'll go off on the hunt with him. I'll try to kill the deer." The torment on his face was an incredible thing. "Last chance," Archie, Jr., said. "Last chance for me. If I don't do it tomorrow — I'll never be able to. I've got to get him off my back. I can't take him for another day. For another hour. I'm going to kill a deer. Because if I don't ... I'll go out of my mind. I'll run a razor blade across my throat. If I had any guts ... I'd have done it long before now. I really would. I should have. I really should have. Oh, God — the relief ... just to get him off my back ... the relief ...."

Pierce knew at that moment what it was all about. He understood the trips to the psychiatrist. The torrential babble from across the room. The safety valve starting to come apart. The repressions of twenty-one years churning and straining and screaming to be let out.

Then Archie, Jr., closed his mouth. And then he closed his eyes. He just stood there near the fireplace, head down, fists clenched. Only one visible movement — the thin white scar pulsating very slowly. Beat. Beat. Beat. But silence.

"Good night, Archie," Pierce said.

He walked out of the room and closed the door behind him. He crossed the giant entrance hall and started up the steps to the guest room above. He wondered, as he walked, how many other scars Archie, Jr., had engraved on his body. Pistol butts, knuckles, and God knew what else. And then later, lying sleepless in his bed, consciously fending off a nightmare by his wakefulness, he thought of all the bullet holes that Colonel Dittman had left behind in fifty-odd years of killing. The bullet holes. The torn flesh. The punctured bodies. And his son's scars. All the trophies of the kill.

Pierce would remember years afterward (and quite mercifully) fragments of the next day's nightmare. Swatches of the mosaic separated by imposed blackouts. The nightmare had waited through the long night of rain, and began to show itself at breakfast the following morning. Pierce had found hunting clothes draped neatly over a chair in his bedroom. He had put them on, not really knowing why.

At breakfast Colonel Dittman had been thin-lipped, silent, and taciturn. Archie, Jr., had joined them at the last moment for a quick cup of black coffee. Not six words of dialogue were spoken through the silent aftermath of breakfast. And then the hike out into the fields twenty minutes afterward. And this, being part of the nightmare, was never a whole picture in Pierce's memory. Left behind were small shreds of the chronology.

He remembered starting down a ridge, his rifle a strange, foreign, unfriendly accouterment. In front of him Archie, Jr., walked methodically behind his father. He had held his gun at port like an infantryman on patrol. But Colonel Dittman had walked in slow, measured strides, head high, eyes alert. Occasionally he had delivered up tidbits of hunting expertise. After a rain was a great time to hunt. Deer came out to enjoy the good weather, as well as to feed. Down below, in a narrow, winding canyon, was chamiza and wild cherry — favorite food of the intended victim. And deer didn't like wind. It was normal that they would get on the lee of a hill, and whitetails, living as they did in comparatively heavy cover, would often sneak out, move a short distance, then stop to wait you out — or else cut back in a circle behind you.

Every few moments Colonel Dittman would throw out a terse clue — a short machine-gun burst of knowledge. But, Pierce had noted, he would always look at his son — gauging, inventorying, challenging, as if to say, "Sometime soon now."

Twenty minutes later they had seen their deer. A giant-antlered majestic-looking creature standing stock still in a clump of low trees.

Unbidden and with a strange sense of shame, Pierce felt his heart beat faster. What was it? That fundamental primeval excitement that comes to the creature on the hunt? Some ingrained awareness of man's elemental pastime — his sovereign right to perform murder under the protection of a state-issued hunting license? Whatever it was, Pierce had known then that there was something about the stalking that sent a little tremor through his body. And the feeling was, God help him, not unpleasant.

Dittman, Sr., looked back at his son and whispered, "You place your shot, Archie, so you kill or anchor him at once. Line up the front leg as the upright part of a 'T' and the backline is the cross part. Aim to break the shoulder just above the middle of the body. That way you'll bring him down quick."

Archie, Jr., raised his rifle, and Pierce noted with surprise that there was nothing hesitant about the boy then.

Again the Colonel's whisper. "If you shoot high, Archie, you'll break his back. And if you shoot behind, you'll get the lungs. A low shot can hit the heart, but if you're high in front, you get the neck. Make it a clean kill, Archie."

The boy nodded and started to sight down into the canyon. The deer remained stock still, frozen there. It was as if he'd already taken his bullet and was down there on display, stuffed. Dead. An item out of Disneyland.

But Pierce, incredibly enough, was not prepared for the noise. A loud explosion. A little wisp of smoke out of the breech of Archie Jr.'s gun.

And down below, the deer leaped high, then ran.

He did it, by God, Pierce thought — after his shock at the noise. The boy had actually fired at a target and hit it. He was not prepared, however, for the look on Colonel Dittman's face — the twisted, contorted, bestial look — the quivering thin lips, the suddenly bright maniacal eyes.

"You punk," the Colonel said. "You dumb, stupid punk. You got him in the Goddamned lungs. That's where you got him. I'm sure of it."

And then Archie, Jr., simply put down the rifle gently. He looked at it for a moment, then turned his head and vomited on the ground — a long, rasping, ugly noise.

Colonel Dittman reached him in one stride, grabbing him by the front of his hunting jacket. "Now, you weak son of a bitch — we're going to have to follow his tracks. We'll have to check the blood drops and find out just where you got him."

It was a moment before Pierce realized he'd let loose of his own gun and it was embedded in brush at his feet. He felt disoriented. It was as if he were watching a three-ring circus, each act demanding his attention. The boy was sick. His father looked as if he were about to kill him; and there was also some language floating about blood and tracks, and some garbled phrases that Pierce couldn't understand but wanted to.

"Colonel," Pierce said, "he got the deer —"

Dittman, still clutching the boy, looked toward Pierce. "We'll have to find out where he got hit," he said. "We'll be able to tell from the blood. Blood from the body and limbs is kind of medium in color, and it usually means just a superficial wound. Lung blood is light-colored — and that means a long hunt. The Goddamned deer could be alive for hours." Then he jerked his head back toward his son. "I told you. A clean kill. You know what that means? A clean kill. That means you don't butcher him. Jesus, I could have ordered an animal for you. Tied him down and let you go at him with an ax. It's the same Goddamned thing."

Dittman was actually screaming then. For a moment it appeared that he might put those hands of his around the boy's neck.

But it was part of the dreamlike quality of the whole scene, Pierce noted, that Archie, Jr., simply lifted his hands, pushed them

gently against his father's, and broke free. Like a judo expert knowing that precise point on the opponent's body where the touch of
a finger could nullify all that strength and frustrate all that rage.
For Colonel Dittman simply dropped his hands and watched his
son turn and start to walk away back up toward the top of the
ridge. Slow motion, Pierce observed. That boneless walk. Shoulders
hunched. Head bent. The walk of defeat. Interim salvation only.
The short breather before destruction. The walk was so humble and
humiliated and so accepting of what had to be failure.

"Look at him." Colonel Dittman's voice was like the rasping
shriek of metal against metal. "First he butchers, then he walks
away. In your life, Mr. Pierce, have you ever seen anything like it?"

"He tried, Colonel," Pierce said in a soft voice. "God but he
tried." He looked up, to see Dittman staring at him.

"And that's all it takes, huh? You're not a helluva lot different
than he is. You're willing to go halves on anything. You've got frigging cheap tastes, Mr. Pierce. Altogether frigging cheap tastes."

They were the last words Pierce ever heard Dittman, Sr., utter.
He had vague remembrances of returning to the house by himself
— a stumbling, directionless walk that almost accidentally brought
him back to where he had begun. He had another vague recollection of finding himself in his bedroom, packing his overnight case,
taking off his hunting clothes and putting them back on the chair.
There was something distasteful about these clothes. Their feel and
their touch. It was as if they'd been exposed to a plague and they
crawled with living virus. If Pierce could have burned them, that
would have been the first thing he would have done.

Moments later — or perhaps an hour — he remembered hearing the front door open down below and then shut with a thudding
echo, like some giant footstep. He could never remember his walk
down the steps or moving across the front hall toward the Hunting
Room. But he would never forget opening the doors. He had heard
the sound of hammering. It had been loud and persistent, and it

seemed to have gone on for a long time. But the frozen moment — the one that would embed itself in his mind's eye and would repeat itself night after night when he would wake screaming, was what he saw at that moment.

There was the face of Archie, Jr., and he was smiling. He held a hammer in a bleeding hand, and there was something indistinct on his face — like a photograph out of focus. And then there was the thing on the wall. The apparition. The close-cropped white hair. The nail protruding out of the mouth on which rested the upper row of teeth. And the eyes still registering their disbelief. Colonel Dittman's eyes. Disbelief and protest. Those eyes seemed to look past his son and seek out Pierce. Mr. Pierce, they seemed to say. Wrong victor. Wrong vanquished. Wrong trophy in the wrong room. And Pierce, with the insane rationality that comes when a man's reason is being slowly chipped away, wanted to ask: How can you bleed so much? Just a head. How can it continue to bleed? How can it so redden a wall? And where could Archie, Jr., have found a nail that long — one that could reach through a mouth and then through a brain and have enough left to embed itself into a walnut wall?

"Mr. Pierce —" Archie Jr.'s voice was soft and yet prideful. "Take a look at this, Mr. Pierce. I got him about an hour ago. And I got him with his own gun. He was so surprised, he didn't even argue. I just took it from him. And when he started to run — I brought him down with one shot. Right in the middle of the old 'T' zone. He flew off the ground about five feet. He was dead before he came down."

Archie, Jr., looked up at the trophy on the wall. "An altogether clean kill, Mr. Pierce. A damned clean kill. And *I* got him. Best shot I ever made. You should have been there. You should have seen him."

Then Archie, Jr., stepped back and let the hammer fall to the floor.

Pierce had some recollection that it had made a noise. He had a further recollection that a servant had suddenly appeared through the open door and screamed. And the scream persisted, as whoever it was ran through the house — a fading siren.

They stood there in the room, just the two of them. Archie, Jr., and Pierce. Both looked at the long row of trophies. Colonel Dittman had a smaller head than the lion, Pierce noted — and he had no horns like the gazelle, and his teeth weren't as sharp and pointed as the baboon's. But there was a look of intelligence in the dead eyes. A look of reason. As befitting a superior beast. And it was quite remarkable, Pierce further noted, as his own control began to crumple away around the edges. It took man to kill man. And that proved something. Superiority, perhaps. Manifest destiny — that kind of thing. His worthiness as an adversary. Oh, yes, it most certainly proved something about the preeminence of man.

Then Pierce closed his eyes. His own brain could take no more. He could fill it with only so much horror, and then it overflowed. But as it was, his eyes didn't close quickly enough. There was one more image he would carry with him: the Great Chief's son walking proudly around the room — chuckling, gurgling, and mouthing little sounds; and leaving a criss-cross pattern of bloody footprints that seemed strangely symmetrical, and in *that* room — altogether proper.

THEY'RE TEARING DOWN
TIM RILEY'S BAR

At precisely three o'clock Harvey Doane erupted from his office
— his intense, hairless college-boy face crowned by the mop of
Edwardian hair. He looked briefly down the long row of secretaries
at their desks and listened briefly to the collective sounds of forty
typewriters mixed with the monotonous voices of the two switchboard operators at the far end of the corridor who plugged in and
plugged out and repeated over and over again, "Pritikin's Plastic
Products."

On Harvey Doane's door the gold lettering identified him as
"Assistant Sales Director," and in Harvey Doane's personal view,
neither the title nor the function fitted his consummate talents.

He saw Mr. Pritikin come out of his office and pause by his
secretary's desk. He noted, satisfied, the open door to Randy Lane's
office next door. The room was empty, and Jane Alcott, Lane's secretary, looked nervously from Pritikin to the clock, and then over
toward Doane.

Alcott was one of the few broads on the floor who had a fix on
Doane and read him for the aggressive, climbing, and altogether
merciless young bastard that he was.

Doane sauntered over to her, looked up toward the clock,
checked briefly that Pritikin was still there, and then said, in an
overloud voice, "Randy not back yet?"

Jane Alcott bit her lower lip, looked nervously toward Pritikin, and tried to keep the naked dislike she felt for Doane out of her voice. "He had several meetings outside."

Doane took another quick, surreptitious look toward Pritikin to make certain he was listening. "With several outside martinis," he said, chuckling and wiggling a finger toward the open door to Lane's empty office. He gave Miss Alcott an extravagant wink, then lowered his eyes in humble embarrassment as Mr. Pritikin approached. Beautiful, he thought, as he forced himself to look surprised that Pritikin had overheard, or that Pritikin was even there. Three o'clock, Lane's still out, establish the drinking, and let Pritikin see him there, functioning while his superior tippled away the afternoon. Beautiful.

Mr. Pritikin had a heavy, semifrog face with drooping, thick-lidded eyes, and when angry or impatient, he talked through semi-clenched teeth. "When is Mr. Lane due back?" he asked Miss Alcott. "I have to talk to him about the Carstair order."

"I'm right on top of that myself, Mr. Pritikin," Doane offered, much too quickly. "I can give you any information you need, sir."

Pritikin looked at him briefly. "I thought Lane was handling that."

Miss Alcott had her mouth open to speak, but Harvey Doane had already rolled his artillery through the breach. "I've pretty much taken that over," Doane said. "Got a full report on my desk. If you'll just give me a minute, sir, I'll get it."

He turned quickly and trotted back to his office.

Jane Alcott felt her cheeks burn. She sensed Pritikin staring at her. Her hands shook, and she tried to use them to rearrange her desk — a flowerpot, six inches to the left, pencils straightened out into a line, typing paper smoothed out, and then her hands just lay there with nothing further to do.

"Where is he, Miss Alcott?" Pritikin asked in a softer tone.

"He ... well ... he mentioned some meetings outside, Mr. Pritikin —"

"I've no doubt," Pritkin said. "Most of his business of late seems to *be* outside." He turned away, then looked at her over his shoulder. "Tell him I want to see him when he gets back."

He started back toward his own office as Doane came dog-trotting out, a sheaf of papers in his hand, looking like a cross between a cocker spaniel and a vulture. "Mr. Pritikin — I have the Carstair material right here, sir."

Pritikin paused by his office door. "Bring it in here," he said.

And Harvey Doane, anchor man on the Olympic Back-Knifing Squad, headed toward him and into his office.

"Mr. Pritikin," Miss Alcott called.

Pritikin turned back toward her from his office door. "Yes, Miss Alcott."

Miss Alcott knew she was blushing, and could do nothing about it. "Today is Mr. Lane's twenty-fifth anniversary," she said, trying to keep her voice even.

Pritikin frowned at her. "His anniversary? That man's been a widower for twenty years —"

"Twenty-five years with the company," Miss Alcott tried to say without emotion.

"I wasn't aware of that," Pritikin said. Again he turned to enter his office, and again her voice stopped him.

"I only broached it, sir," she said, "because ... well ... because maybe someone in the firm took him to lunch or something. Just a little celebration."

Pritikin's nod conveyed nothing. He simply moved into his office, where the eager Doane stood in the middle of the room, and closed the door.

Miss Alcott waited for a moment, then rose and entered Randolph Lane's office. She moved hurriedly over to his phone, dialed an outside line, waited for a moment. "Antoine," she asked, "is Mr. Lane there? Did he have lunch there? But he's not there now? Well, if he should come in — will you tell him to please get in touch with his office right away? Yes. Thank you. This is his secretary."

She cradled the phone for a moment, then let her eyes wander over Lane's desk. There was a picture of his wife, very young; a doodled calender with the day's date circled and starred, a scribbled notation on it which read "Quarter of a Century." And as her eyes quickly inventoried the desk, she saw the whiskey bottle protruding from an open side drawer. She closed the drawer quickly, tidied up the desk, then glanced toward the door to see Randolph Lane standing there.

He looked as he always looked after a wet lunch. Tie at half-mast, normally rumpled shirt collar even more rumpled, thinning hair hanging over his eyes — much-too-tight suit, buttoned in front with difficulty. And the eyes ... the tired eyes ... grave but good-humored.

He bowed as he closed the door behind him. "How do you do, madam. Could I interest you in a line of plastics?"

Miss Alcott felt like a woman who'd lost her child on the beach and then found him again. First she wanted to hug him — then belt him. "It's three o'clock," she said.

Lane brought his wristwatch to within an inch of one eye, focusing with difficulty on the dial. "Why, so it is," he said. "Inexorable time in its flight."

He walked across the room over to his desk. "But what the hell," he said, "this is a special day."

"I know," Miss Alcott said softly.

Lane looked up at her, squinting. "On this day, Miss Alcott," he announced, "twenty-five years ago, having conquered Europe for General Eisenhower and President Truman, I doffed my khaki — and I enlisted in the cause of Pritikin's Plastic Products. Twenty-five years, Miss Alcott. A quarter of a century." He moved around the desk and sat down, blinking a little. "So what the hell," he said, grinning. "If a man can't get a little sauced on this kind of an anniversary — where the hell does that leave the flag and motherhood?" He looked briefly around his desk, then across it to Miss Alcott. "Any messages?" he asked.

Miss Alcott tried to keep the concern out of her voice. "Mr. Pritikin was looking for the Carstair order. Mr. Doane took it in to him." She tried not to sound accusative, but the word "Doane" got spat out. Her dislike of Harvey Doane was no secret. From his carefully curled locks to the bottom of his bell-bottom trousers, he was a conniving little bastard, and both she and Lane knew it.

Lane smiled at her — a smile slightly worn around the edges. "Mr. Doane took it in to him," he repeated. He grinned again and shook his head back and forth. "Johnny-on-the-spot Doane! With assistants like him — who needs assassins?" He leaned back in his chair and closed his eyes, arms folded behind his head.

Lane shrugged. "What the hell difference?" Then he smiled again. "You see before you, Miss Alcott, a man much too old and set in his ways, and at the moment a little too deep in his cups, to give battle to the young Turk in the cubicle to my immediate left."

That young Turk, Miss Alcott thought but did not say, is made up of one-half brass and one-half elbow, and his mission in life is to ace you right out of the picture. She gnawed on her lip. "He's ... he's damned anxious for your job," she said. "You're aware of that, aren't you?"

Lane's smile was wistful. He nodded, then turned in the chair to look out the window behind him. "You know where I've been the last hour, Miss Alcott? I've been watching them tear down Tim Riley's Bar." Again he swiveled around in his chair. "That doesn't mean anything to you, does it?"

"Should it?"

"Nope. It's an ancient, ugly, son-of-a-bitch eyesore," he said, "which will now be turned into a twenty-story bank building with an underground parking lot — and it'll have glass walls and fluorescent lighting and high-speed self-service elevators and piped-in music in the lobby." He leaned forward, elbows now on the desk. "And a year from now," he continued, "nobody will remember that Tim Riley had a bar on that corner. Or that he sold beer for a nickel a glass. Or that he had snooker tables in the back. Or that he had a big nickelodeon, and you got three Glenn Millers for a dime."

He laughed, looked briefly at his late wife's picture, then remained silent for a moment. "And while I was standing there," he said, looking up at his secretary, "with all the other sidewalk superintendents, the thought occurred to me that there should be some kind of ceremony. Maybe a convocation of former beer drinkers and Timothy Riley patrons to hang a wreath or say a few words."

He rose, and his smile was vague and wistful. There he stood in the garbage dump of the past two decades, looking across the wreckage of twenty lonely years, and he knew — clearly, rationally, achingly — all the martinis on God's earth couldn't bring it back; the objects of a man's love weren't pawned for a future desperate moment — they were buried and could only be mourned.

"Farewell, Timothy Riley's Bar," Lane said softly. "Home of the nickel beer. Snooker emporium. Repository of Bluebird records, three for a dime. We honor you and your passing. Farewell. Farewell, Timothy Riley — and terraplanes and rumbleseats and saddle shoes and Helen Forrest and the Triple-C camps and Andy Hardy and Lum 'n' Abner and the world-champion New York Yankees! Rest in peace, you age of innocence — you beautiful, serene, carefree, pre-Pearl Harbor, long summer night. We'll never see your likes again."

He felt the familiar ache — the lonely air pocket inside of him — and he wished at that moment that he hadn't had so much to drink. He finally raised his head, took a deep breath, grinned at her. "There is nothing," he said lightly, "nothing as remotely embarrassing as a middle-age crying jag! And I humbly ask your forgiveness for having been exposed to one."

Jane Alcott tried to say something. She wanted to tell him that he could deliver up crying jags, four-letter Anglo-Saxon words, and anything else that might please him. All she could do was smile at him, and she hoped — oh, God, she hoped — he'd understand.

"Just bear with me, will you, Miss Alcott?" Lane said, seeing the look on her face. "They knocked down the walls of Timothy Riley's Bar. And as silly and as Goddamned sentimental as it sounds — I lost something."

Harvel Doane's voice intruded into the room like a race car slamming into a bleacher full of spectators. "What do you say, sport?" Doane said, entering the room. "Have a good lunch?"

Lane and Miss Alcott exchanged a look. She very quickly moved past Doane and out to her desk, closing the door behind her.

Lane sat back down in his chair. "The question again? My lunch? Dandy."

Doane walked across the room and sat on the corner on the desk. He examined his nails. "I took the Carstair stuff into the old man. He was kind of anxious."

"Good of you," Lane said.

Doane looked at him ever so briefly. "And I added a few embellishments. Hope you don't mind."

Lane shrugged. "Be my guest."

Doane was opening the can, and he was three quarters of the way — slight change in tone now. Just a little incisive. "And the sales pitch you had in the opening ... I had to touch that up quite a bit." This time he look straight at Lane, waiting for the explosion.

"Touch away, lad," Lane said affably, "touch away."

There was a silence. "You putting me on?" Harvey Doane asked.

Lane pointed to himself. "Me? Put you on? Why would I want to do that?"

Doane stood up from the desk. "Usually when I try to be a little independent — you step on me."

Lane studied him very carefully. "Usually," he said very softly, "when you try to be a little independent — you're also a little too flamboyant, a little too artsy-craftsy and a little too dishonest." he leaned across the desk. "I put my foot on you, Mr. Doane, to keep you within ten feet of Mother Earth. I know you're one helluva hot-shot peddler — but if you don't get mildly restrained along the way, you'll be selling Brighton Beach sand and calling it moon rocks."

Doane's smile looked like a puckered-up fist. "Takes awhile, doesn't it?" he said.

"To do what?"

"To get a rise out of you. Ferdinand the bull."

Lane cocked his head, studying the younger man. "My son, the matador." He pointed to Doane. "Young Master Doane who simply has to draw blood before the six-o'clock whistle, or the day is shot down." Again he pointed to Doane. "Give yourself a point. You pricked me. You got the old bull riled." He stood up and moved out from behind the desk. "I would ask that you keep one thing in mind, Mr. Doane. There is still a pecking order around here. You're still outranked. You're still my assistant." His voice rose as he stood a half an arm's length away, so close to Doane that he could smell his cologne. "And until such day as you are no longer my assistant — I want you to keep your frigging, bloody, hungry little hands off my desk, away from my business, and —"

The sound of the door opening stopped him abruptly. Both men turned, to see Mr. Pritikin standing there. He looked from one to the other. "Is this a private altercation?" he asked. "Or may I involve myself?"

As he turned to close the door, he saw Miss Alcott at her desk, white-faced and frightened. He very grimly and pointedly closed the door, then turned to face the two men again. "Well, Doane?"

Doane turned into a West Point plebe, standing straight, tall, and honorable. "It really wasn't anything, sir." His voice was low, like a man dying bravely and uncomplainingly from a dum-dum bullet wound. "Mr. Lane was simply reminding me of his seniority." Try that, Randolph, he thought to himself. Keep the knife in and squirm — or pull it out and bleed to death.

"Perhaps Mr. Lane should be reminded," Pritikin said, "that seniority doesn't come from merely putting in time. Not on this ball club." He looked meaningfully toward Lane. "I judge a man by his current record. Not last season's batting average."

Harvey Doane's sigh was almost audible. It was working. The Doane Master Plan for Ultimate Advancement was zooming down the track on schedule.

Randy Lane simply smiled. There was no bite in his voice. And no defense. "What have you done for me lately, huh?" he said.

Pritikin, like Doane, needed opposition. When he took on a man, it had to be nose to nose. Belligerence he could shout down, and weakness he could tear to pieces. But blandness ... that was another thing.

Pritikin felt the anger rise "Precisely," he agreed. And what you've done for us lately isn't very damned much, Lane. You've put in time, but not much else. Protracted lunch hours — considerable martini drinking — and precious damned little mustard cut!" He nodded toward Doane. "Candidly, Lane, your assistant here has left you whinnying at the starting gate."

Again Lane grinned and waggled his finger at the heavyset, red-faced man. "Mr. Pritikin," he said gently, "you're mixing your metaphors. You want this baseball — or horse racing?"

Pritikin did everything but shake. "I want this *understood* is what I want. Your performance, Lane, has deteriorated. Your sales have slipped. Your entire attitude has become sloppy."

Harvey Doane held his breath. It was coming. It had to be coming.

"I suggest a trial period," Pritikin said, "during which both you and Mr. Doane will share the director's spot. He'll no longer be answerable to you. You can consult each other, but any ideas he has of his own, he's free to follow. That understood?"

Lane nodded. His voice was altogether affable. "Clearly."

Doane stood stock still. The humble hero just getting his Congressional Medal.

Pritikin moved to the door, then turned. He knew then, as he had pretty much guessed for the past year or so, that Lane was on his way out. He was sufficiently lousy as a judge of men not to realize that Harvey Doane on his best day was a plastic counterpart to a legal ambulance chaser. But though insensitive, he was not a vindictive man nor a cruel man. He coughed slightly at the door, looked a little indecisive, then blurted it out. "Incidentally, Lane — I'm reminded that this is your twenty-fifth year with the company. This little unpleasantry notwithstanding — I just wanted you to know that you have my congratulations."

He waited for a response. Lane said nothing. Pritikin opened the door and walked out, closing it behind him.

Lane walked over to his desk, opened up the drawer, and took out the bottle; then he looked across at Doane, who stood there looking uncomfortable.

"Something else, was there?" Lane asked. "Like maybe a funeral oration?"

Doane wet his lips. "I ... I just wanted to assure you, sport, that I had nothing to do with this. It was just as much a surprise to me as it is to you."

Lane nodded. "Honest?"

"Believe it," Doane said.

Lane nodded again. "He just called you in, pinched you on the cheek, and promoted you — and you were shocked out of your skivvies — is that it?" He stared at Doane. "Young Mr. Doane," he said very softly, "why don't we level with one another? I'm on the way down, you're on the way up — and we're just passing each other in midair. I'm looking at a threat — and you're looking at an obstacle. And that's a lousy basis for any friendly mutual back scratching!"

It occurred to Doane at this moment that Randy Lane, age forty-five plus, and halfway to lushdom, could still be a formidable opponent. He tried to look humble and sound ingratiating. "Look, Randy," he said, "there's no reason why we can't work together —"

"No reason in the world," Lane replied, "except that we don't complement each other. I'm not a competitor, young Mr. Doane. I wear gloves. I observe ancient and archaic amenities. I'm an old-fashioned slob. *The fancy knifing I leave to commandos like you.*" He sat down in his desk chair. "Now, a favor. Would you please to get the hell out of here?"

Frozen-faced, Doane turned on his heel and walked stiffly out of the office, slamming the door.

Lane uncorked the bottle, looked around for a glass, and failing, tilted the bottle to his mouth and swallowed down just enough to make his eyes water. Then he corked up the bottle, put it back into his desk drawer.

There was a knock on the door, and Miss Alcott opened it and entered.

It was odd, Lane thought, as he looked up at her. She couldn't have been over twenty-five — bright, stacked and altogether lovely. She'd been with him for a little over a year. How could someone who looked like that grow so fiercely loyal to someone like him?

"Can I get you something?" she asked.

Lane had to laugh. "Why, indeed. I had in mind a gold watch. Properly inscribed for this anointed day. Something like 'Well done, good and faithful servant.'" He shook his head. "Short of that, my love, I don't think there is anything you can get me."

Miss Alcott took another step into the office. "You know," she said a little nervously, "on an anointed day like this, a guy shouldn't have to spend the evening alone. I've got a steak in the freezer saved for a special occasion. I've got two large Idahos suitable for baking, and a great salad dressing I make myself." There was a silence. "What do you say?"

Lane smiled. "I say — that you're a very dear young lady. I say thank you … but no thank you."

"Why not?" she asked, disappointed.

Lane shrugged. "The syndrome of the twenty-five year man who didn't get his gold watch. He's too full of himself and too sorry for himself, and he makes lousy company." Then he smiled. "Another time, maybe?"

"Sure," Miss Alcott said.

"Miss Alcott," Lane called to her as she turned.

She looked back at him.

"You're a helluva good lady. I mean that."

Jane Alcott felt something rise inside of her. It was female and mixed up and impossible to isolate and understand. She'd been feeling it more and more with Randy Lane for the better part of six months. It was affection, sympathy, compassion, and something far more physical than she wanted to admit. "I guess," she said, "it's because I work for a helluva good guy. And *I* mean that."

She turned and left him sitting there.

The top three floors of the four-story building had already been knocked down, and only Tim Riley's bar remained standing — faded and ancient brick, broken and boarded windows with a sign hanging askew. "Tim Riley's Bar" was spelled out in weathered, barely legible printing.

Randy Lane sat on a fire hydrant, staring up at the sign — thinking how dejected and forlorn it looked and how the wood slats covering the big window looked like a giant eyepatch. He very carefully got up from the hydrant and took an unsteady walk over to the front door. This too, was crisscrossed with wooden boards, and there was just about six inches of space that he could peer through into the interior. All he could make out was the dark outline of the full-length bar and nothing else. He heard footsteps on the sidewalk and turned to see the bulky blue-coated figure of McDonough, the cop — the genial County Mayo face much more wrinkled than he remembered.

"They're closed," McDonough said.

Lane nodded and again peered through the wood slats. "Don't I know it."

The policeman studied Lane, then looked up past the sign to the empty sky where there had once been a building. "I know how you feel," he said gently. "First arrest I ever made was inside Tim Riley's. Two guys fighting over whether Carl Hubbell could throw harder'n Lefty Gomez — and if that don't date me, Randy, I'll join Tim Riley under the sod."

Lane felt memories of his own welling up. "First date I ever had," he said, "was right here with my wife. When her father heard about it, he almost had a stroke."

McDonough smiled. "Katie," he said softly. "Katie Donovant. As if I didn't remember her. She was a lovely, lovely lady, Randy."

He felt the ache again. The air pocket. "That she was," he said. Then he grinned as other recollections took over. "And when I came back from the service — they had a surprise party for me in there. My God, McDonough — you were there. My train was late, remember? By the time I got here, my old man was sound asleep in the corner."

McDonough laughed. "And don't I remember *that*. But I'll say this for him: he could drink a keg of that stuff. And many's the night I sat with him while he did it. And while *I* did it."

The two men both laughed and then stared toward the darkened interior.

McDonough studied Lane's profile and couldn't help but notice the seedy look to his clothes and the way his shoulders slumped. "Things going well for you, Randy?" he asked.

Lane nodded. "I'm forty-six years old. I'm six years younger than my father was when he died."

McDonough put a hand on his shoulder. "When I first saw you in here, Randy, I had a spring in my step, arches in my feet, and my ambition in life was to capture Al Capone. Then one morning I woke up ... and I knew I'd run out of vinegar. All I wanted was Epsom salt. So I just walk a little slower and I pray for quiet nights. And I just keep reminding myself that I'm flat-footed and slow as molasses — but I'm still a whole helluva lot faster'n Al Capone is." He winked and grinned. "Look after yourself, Randy."

He turned and with his flat-footed policeman gait continued down the sidewalk, swinging his club in the manner of policemen fifty years before.

Randy Lane watched him walk off and disappear around the corner. Then once again he looked up at the Tim Riley sign. It occurred to him he could go to the next block and the cocktail lounge that stayed open until four. But a younger crowd usually gathered there. They played rock music on the juke, and it was so damned noisy. But he had no choice except perhaps to go home. Home. The empty apartment. The late show on television. The TV dinner. But what the hell. Tim Riley's wasn't serving that night. So he turned and was about to walk away when he heard it. Faintly, as if from far off, the singing voices of "For He's a Jolly Good Fellow" — indistinct, but growing louder. He retraced his steps over to the door and once again peered into the interior of the darkened bar.

A car drove by, and briefly its headlights shone over Lane's shoulder to illuminate the inside. Then the car pulled around the corner, taking its lights with it, and once again the cobwebbed musty interior was dark.

Or was it?

For a while Randy Lane stood there peering through the slats. He suddenly made out the outlines of people. They looked fuzzy, as if seen through gauze. But they were there. People holding up mugs of beer. They looked like slow-motion characters of an ancient film. But there was Tim himself behind the bar. And there was his father in the corner, blinking his eyes.

Lane stepped back and sent his foot in a swinging arc to smash against the wooden slats. One of them cracked. Another flew off one of its nails. He yanked at it furiously, pulled it aside, kicked again at the one remaining, and then smashed the full weight of his body against sagging door and entered Tim Riley's bar.

Just for a moment ... just for a single moment ... he saw a banner stretched across the room which read, "Welcome Home, Randy." And in that moment the voices were loud and the faces recognizable. His father. Tim Riley. Even McDonough was there — a very young cop. And something surged inside Randy Lane. A joy ... an excitement ... a sense of satisfaction, being where he belonged. But as he turned toward his father, the room went dark and empty. Cobwebs and wires from dismantled fixtures and a cracked mirror were all he could make out in the darkness. He stumbled over a broken, overturned chair as he turned and moved back toward the front door. Before leaving he turned once again to survey the room. His loneliness had been a dull, formless thing, and he'd learned to carry it with him. But now he felt the sudden sharp, jabbing pain of something beyond loneliness; some overwhelming anguish almost impossible to bear. He suddenly felt lost and bewildered, as if something ... something important and integral — had just eluded him.

He walked very slowly out of Tim Riley's bar, hesitated for a moment, then headed for the cocktail lounge down the street on the next block. He'd sit at the bar, trying to ignore the nuzzling kids and the blaring rock and the late-night bimbos who would inventory him then move away to a richer pasture. A richer-looking guy and a younger one. And he'd drink just enough to dull the pain and forget the air pocket. And maybe ... just maybe ... by the dawn's early light he could forget Tim Riley's bar and all the love that went with it.

Shortly after 9:00 A.M. the following day, Miss Alcott stood in front of Mr. Blodgett, personnel director of Pritikin's Plastic Products.

He was a short, fastidious, fussy little man who seemed always to be behind time and rushing to catch up.

He looked up as she arrived at his desk, briefly checked her, then sorted out some papers on his desk. "You have a change in assignment," he announced.

Miss Alcott caught her breath. "A change in assignment?"

"Correct. We're moving you."

"From where to where?" she asked.

Blodgett managed a smile. "Relax, Miss Alcott. We're not sending you to a frontier outpost. Just about eight feet to your left. You'll join Mr. Doane as of next Monday morning."

He reshuffled the papers, looked at her briefly, gave her a nod of dismissal, then started to jot down notes on a pad. He tried to ignore the fact that she remained there. He looked up again. "Something else?" Then he frowned. She looked white-faced, ill. "Are you all right, Miss Alcott?"

"Did you say Doane?" she asked.

Blodgett nodded. "His secretary — Miss Trevor — has turned in her notice. She's getting married, I believe. Anyway, she'll be leaving us. So you'll assume her duties." Why, he thought, did the woman just stand there? She was supposed to be such a good secretary — didn't she understand this altogether simple and quite irrevocable move? He looked up at her impatiently. "Was there something else, Miss Alcott?"

"Mr. Blodgett," Jane Alcott said, "what about Mr. Lane?"

Blodgett looked at her blankly. "Mr. Lane?"

She nodded. "I've been with him for over a year."

Blodgett put the pencil in his mouth. "I'm not sure what the arrangement will be. You'll have a replacement, of course, but for the moment I'm told that Mr. Doane will need you as of Monday morning. Requested you personally, as a matter of fact."

"What if I don't want to work for Mr. Doane?"

Blodgett blinked, surprised. "And what's that supposed to mean?"

"It's supposed to mean that he does everything but wear track shoes. He's got five sets of hands. He pinches fannies, and he doesn't happen to be fit to shine Mr. Lane's shoes!"

Blodgett threw the pencil down on his desk. "Regrettably," he said, "in my capacity as personnel director I've neither the time nor the inclination to listen to your personal assessments of the executives of this organization. I'll have to put it to you bluntly, Miss Alcott. You'll either report for work with Mr. Doane on Monday morning — or you'll report to the cashier this afternoon to pick up your severance pay. Now, which will it be, please? I'm very busy."

She looked at that moment no longer angry, and incredibly young. "Does ... Mr. Lane know?" she half-whispered.

"I'm sure someone has seen fit to tell him," Blodgett said, again turning to the papers on his desk. And when he looked up moments later, Miss Alcott had left.

She got on the elevator and went back to her floor. As she moved down the corridor of desks, she saw a group of giggling girls surrounding Doane's secretary. There were gift wrappings thrown about and "oohs" and "aahs" of delight as silver things shown on her desk. One or two of the girls looked at Jane Alcott sideways as she moved past, and there was some whispering.

Miss Alcott went past her desk and into Lane's office.

He was in his usual position, his chair swiveled around, facing the window. Without looking at her, he held up his hand and wiggled his fingers. "Close the door," he said.

She did so after taking a step into the room.

Still he didn't turn. "If it makes it go down any easier, Jane — I feel a whole lot worse about this than you do."

She felt a catch in her throat. "I seriously doubt that," she said.

Lane very slowly turned around in the chair. "Look," he said, "you've got no choice." There was no self-pity in the voice — just a kind of resigned awareness. "You tie yourself to a rocket — or to a groundhog. There's so much handwriting on the walls around here, the whole Goddamned place looks like a gigantic men's room."

"I don't want to work for Doane. It's as simple as that."

Lane studied her. "So give it a shot. If there's anybody on this earth who can put him down and keep him in line — it's you."

She waited for a moment, hoping there would be something else said. When he remained silent, she knew that this was it. "Is that it?" she asked.

Lane smiled at her. "Oh, there's a great deal more to say. A couple of items having to do with how grateful I am for all you've done for me. But unfortunately, I'm cold stone sober now and not given to loquaciousness." Then his smile faded, and his voice sounded intense. "But you know that, don't you, Jane? You know how grateful I am to you."

They looked at one another and they both smiled — the kind of smile friends exchange when one is on the train leaving and the other stands on the platform waving good bye.

Jane Alcott turned and left the office, wondering why the decent guys — the nice guys — the sensitive, gentle, caring guys — were either married or inaccessible. When she got to her desk she started to clear away the drawers. One thing was certain — she'd never work for Harvey Doane.

From the opposite end of the corridor she was vaguely conscious of the secretaries breaking up with parting congratulations to the bride-to-be, Miss Trevor. One of the girls was humming "For He's a Jolly Good Fellow," and as she passed Jane Alcott's desk, her voice carried through to the interior of Lane's office.

He was sitting at his desk and looked up, listening to the passing melody. It reminded him of the previous night. And he sat there pondering. He was not an imaginative man — at least not one given to fantasies around the clock. And it was very odd, he thought — those hallucinations. And it was odder yet that he had felt no fear at all. He supposed that it was *because* they were hallucinations. Not phantoms. Hallucinations made up of wishful thinking and probably his gin-and-vermouth ration. He smiled a little wanly, listening to the tune as it floated by, and when he turned around to face his desk, the hallucinations had returned. It was the old war-surplus roller-top that Pritikin had given him the first week he'd worked there. And the room was bare, and much smaller. And the sound of singing was louder now and came from many voices from outside.

Like a captivated kid moving after the Pied Piper, he rose, crossed the room, and opened the door. What he saw was Pritikin's Plastic Products of twenty-five years ago. There were just two desks outside, and two secretaries, both older women in long skirts. One doubled as a switchboard operator. He remembered her. Harris or Harrison or something like that. He blinked at her, then turned to see Mr. Pritikin come out of his office. Pritikin's hair was black, and he wore a moustache.

He walked directly over to Lane, smiled, patted him on the arm. "Well, sir, what's the first day been like, Randy?" Pritikin asked him.

Lane stared at him and then looked over his shoulder at a calendar on the desk. It read "May, 1945."

Still no fear, but now confusion .... "The first day?" he asked.

Pritikin chuckled. "Just wanted you to know I'm going to keep my eye on you, Randy. You're going to become our number-one salesman. Numero uno! Plastics are going to make it, my boy,

Plastics are going to kill them. And we're right there on the ground floor!"

Lane became conscious of a phone ringing, and one of the women looked up at him after answering it. "Mr. Lane," she said, "phone call for you. It's your wife. Want to get it on your own phone?"

"My wife," Lane whispered. "My wife."

"Yes, sir," the secretary said, smiling.

"My wife," Lane said, much louder as he ran back to his own office. He grabbed the phone as if wanting to devour it. "Honey. Honey, it's Randy," he said, his heart pounding. His wife, Katie. Katie on the other end of the line. Katie back, and a part of his life. Katie —

There was no sound on the other end, and when Lane looked up, the fantasy, or whatever it was, had ended.

Miss Alcott stood at the open door. "Did you call me, Mr. Lane?"

"Call you?" Lane said in a hollow, empty voice.

"I thought I heard you call me."

Lane shook his head, looked briefly at the phone in his hand, then put it back on its cradle.

"Is there anything wrong?" Miss Alcott asked him.

Lane looked at the framed picture of his wife. He touched it tenderly. "No," he said. "No, there's nothing wrong." And as he said it, he knew there was something very wrong. Something infinitely wrong. Something uncorrectable. He was like a man falling down a hillside, scrabbling for a rock or an outgrowth or something to grab onto and stop his fall. And it was too late. Much too late. Katie, he thought, Katie, why in God's name after twenty years ... why can't I stop mourning?

That night Randy Lane went back to Tim Riley's Bar. Very methodically he pulled off the wooden slats that had been replaced across the front door and moved into its interior. He carried with him a beer glass cadged from one of four bars he'd visited that night, and he stood in the middle of the room singing "For He's a Jolly Good Fellow" and waiting ... waiting for it to happen again.

A car pulled up outside. Two policemen got out and carried flashlights into the bar. They played them on Randy Lane, who blinked and smiled, then bowed.

"Good evening, gentlemen," he said happily.

The cops looked at one another. "You better be the night watchman, buddy, or the equivalent," the first cop said to him.

Lane laughed. "Night watchman. Hell, I outrank all the night watchmen in the world. I am late a Sergeant, First Platoon, 'A' Company, 505th Parachute Infantry Regiment, 82nd Airborne Division. That's what *I* am. And I've just recently returned, V.E. Day now being behind us —"

The two cops looked at one another and grinned. Nothing insurmountable here. Just a happy drunk.

The first cop moved over to Lane and took him by the arm. "Why don't you come with us," the cop said, "and we'll celebrate the event? It isn't every day a war ends."

Lane smiled but stood his ground. "I'd like to accommodate you, officer. I really would. But the festivities take place *here*. Very shortly Tim Riley will accompany my old man on the piano while my old man sings 'It's a Long Way to Tipperary.' They will do it in unharmonious harmony ... but what they lack in symmetry — they make up with gusto."

The cop increased the pressure on Lane's arm, and his voice took on a brittle don't-give-me-any-crap quality. "You better come with us, buddy, or —"

At this point McDonough walked into the bar. The second cop shone his flashlight on him, then lowered it when he saw the uniform.

"I'll take care of him," McDonough said. "I know him."

"You know him well enough to explain to him that he can get thirty days apiece for trespassing and being under the influence

— plus tack on ninety more for breaking and entering?" the first cop asked.

"I said I'd take care of him," McDonough said.

The two cops looked at one another, then moved out of the bar. McDonough walked over to Lane, who chuckled and did a little jig, then winked at McDonough and threw his arm around him.

"McDonough, my lad — you're just in time."

McDonough gently removed Lane's arm. "I'm just in time to ride you home, Randy. I'm just goin' off duty, and I got my car parked less than a block away.'"

Lane frowned. "Not gonna stay for the party?" He made a gesture encompassing the dark, empty room.

McDonough's voice was very gentle. "The party's over, Randy."

Lane stared at him. "Over?" He looked around the room again. "Where's everybody gone? Huh? Where's everybody gone?"

McDonough exhaled. "To their respective rewards," he said. "The party's been over for twenty-five years, Randy." He took his arm. "Come on. Let's go home."

Lane looked down at McDonough's hand, then carefully removed it. "Officer McDonough," he said, "this is where it is — right here."

"This is where what it?" McDonough asked.

Lane walked over to the long bar. "The best years of my life," he said over his shoulder." He put his glass down on the bar. "You may want to phone downtown for a psycho squad — or put out a call for reinforcements — but something's happening to me." He turned and peered through the darkness at McDonough. "I keep getting beckoned to by ghosts, Mr. McDonough. Every now and then it's 1945." He grinned. "How do you like them apples?" Then he held up his hand, shutting off McDonough's response. "And if you think that sounds nuts — try this one. I wish to God those ghosts would stick around. They're the best friends I've got. I feel a whole helluva lot more comfortable with them — than I do with all those warm, living flesh-and-blood bodies I ride up and down the elevators with!"

"Randy," McDonough said, "why don't you tell me about it in the car —"

Lane cut him off. "I'll tell you about it right here!" He took a step away from the bar. "I rate something better than I've got. Honest to God I do. Where does it say that every morning of a man's life he's got to Indian-wrestle with every young contender off the sidewalk who's got an itch to climb up a rung?"

He moved over to McDonough and cupped his hands around the policeman's face. "Hey, McDonough ... McDonough," he whispered, "I've put in my time. Understand? I've paid my dues. I shouldn't have to get hustled to death in the daytime ... and die of loneliness every night. That's not the dream. That's not what it's all about."

His voice broke, and his hands fell to his sides, and as he turned away, McDonough noticed that his cheeks were wet.

"Come on, Randy," he said, "I'll drive you home."

Lane nodded. "Sixty-seven Bennett Avenue."

McDonough shook his head. "That's not where you live."

"The hell it isn't."

"That's where you *lived*. Now you live in that high-rise on Norton."

Lane turned to him. "The hell I do. I don't live *there*. I just wash my socks there. I just eat my TV dinners there. That's where I watch Clark Gable and Myrna Loy at midnight. And if I phone Bigelow 666432, I can get waterless cookery, my carpets cleaned or a digital-computerized date whose personality is identical to my own! My God," he said softly, "I live at 67 Bennett Avenue. Two-story white frame. Katie and I bought it six months after we were married."

McDonough studied him, and his voice carried with it an infinite gentleness. "It's empty now, Randy. They're tearing down all the houses on the block. Gonna be an apartment complex."

Lane moved towards the door. "So humor me, McDonough. Drive me there anyway."

McDonough nodded and followed him out onto the sidewalk.

Bennett Avenue was dark, the houses empty and boarded up. A big sign on the edge of the block announced that a construction company was going to turn it into some kind of a garden — a mecca for Senior Citizens.

McDonough parked his car in front of a faded white two-story house with a sagging porch and a yard covered with crab grass, flanked by a broken picket fence.

Lane put down the window and looked out at the "67" still visible over the front door.

"Well?" McDonough asked a little impatiently.

Lane grinned. "Don't build 'em like they used to." He opened up the car door and got out. "I'll walk from here."

McDonough looked nonplussed. "Walk? Look, Randy, I can —"

Lane turned to him. "I can walk from here, McDonough. I'm sober now."

McDonough studied him for another moment. "Okay. But don't go knockin' any doors down. You get a collar on you the next time — I won't be around to help." He put the car in low gear. "Good night, Randy. Get some sleep."

Lane nodded, shut the car door, and threw him a salute.

The police car pulled away from the curb, down the street, and disappeared around a corner.

Lane stood there for a moment, then turned and looked at the house. His eyes moved from window to window, and he heard the sound of voices — Katie's voice — his own — and laughter — and hellos and good-byes — and all the jumbled language of the past — so sweet, so unbearably sweet.

He took a step over to the broken front gate, and Katie's voice hung over the still night air. "Supper's ready, Randy ... Randy, will you wipe your shoes off? You're tracking mud all over the hall carpet

.... Good night, Randy, darling .... Randy, my love .... Randy? ... Randy?"

"Randy." Miss Alcott was standing by her car, staring across at him.

He turned very slowly to face her. The voices ... the ghosts fled. "You lost?" he asked her.

"I thought you might be," she said nervously.

He shook his head. "Hell, no. This is where I live." Then he grinned. "Correction. This is where I *used* to live."

She took a deep breath. "I know it's presumptuous, but ... when you didn't come back from lunch — I got concerned. I remembered you mentioning Tim Riley's Bar. By the time I got there, the policeman was just putting you in his car. I ... I followed —"

Lane was amused and touched. "You followed, huh? Because you were concerned. And Mr. Pritikin? That Sydney Greenstreet of the Plastics Business — was he concerned too?" There was a silence. "Go ahead, Miss Alcott, tell me."

"He was ... upset."

"Upset." He nodded. "I've no doubt. And I'm sure our Mr. Doane put *his* oar in."

"With unholy glee," she said.

"And I'm sure he called Mr. Pritikin's attention to the fact that as of eleven A.M. I had left the premises."

Miss Alcott didn't answer him for a moment; then she nodded. Lane moved away from the picket fence over to her. "I'm on my way out, Janie. You are aware of that, aren't you?"

Again she nodded. Lane shrugged, then looked back toward the house. "Katie and I bought this six months after we were married. Katie was my wife."

Miss Alcott surveyed the faded ruin. "It must have been quite lovely."

"It sure as hell was. It was white with blue shutters and it had a blue tile roof and it had a big fireplace in the living room and it had two extra bedrooms upstairs that we were going to use for the kids." He said it all matter-of-factly. "We had a lot of plans for it."

He moved back over to the broken fence and looked across the crab grass toward the porch. "She died not too long afterward. And there went the plans ... and everything else. Blue shutters," he added disjointedly. "Blue shutters and a blue tile roof."

"You must have loved her very much," Miss Alcott said softly.

Lane smiled. "To the depth and breadth and height my soul can reach." He stopped and turned to her. "Which is from Elizabeth Barrett Browning ... Who is passé ... and is no longer quoted except by lachrymose aging men."

"Have you had anything to eat?" Miss Alcott asked him.

Lane nodded. "I have had sufficient to drink, which more than compensates for what I haven't had to eat. But I thank you," he said smiling. "I thank you for caring. It's very much like you."

Jane Alcott had to shove down the impulse to reach out and touch this man's face ... to fondle him ... to hold him to her. "Randy," she said, this time conjuring up the first name with some difficulty, "do you think I've played Den Mother because I feel sorry for you?" She shook her head. "That's not what it's all about."

He studied her. "Did I ask you what it's all about?"

"I don't just care about you, Randy. I care for you. Not that it makes a damn — but I happen to be in —"

He had moved over to her and gently covered her mouth. "Enough," he said. "Enough already." Then he let his fingers run gently across her cheek. "I am obviously past prime," he said, "but I'm not built out of pig iron. So please don't make it tough for me, huh?"

There was the sudden rolling sound of distant thunder, and then sporadic lightning.

Miss Alcott pointed to her car. "You'll need a ride," she said. "It's going to rain."

Lane looked up at the dark sky and felt the first drops of rain. He started to follow her over to the car, then stopped as she got in, and looked back toward the house.

"What's the matter?" she asked.

"It was raining that night too."

"What night?"

He was remembering. The memory of it came out in words, but spoken to no one in particular. "She'd had a miserable cold. Couldn't shake it. Wouldn't go to a doctor. And when I got home ... there was a neighbor from next door. They'd tried to call me but I wasn't in."

He looked through the car window at Jane sitting here. "Is that a kick?" he asked. "I'm peddling plastics — and my wife is dying."

She leaned across the front seat and opened up the window. "Mr. Lane ... Randy ... listen to me —"

The rain cascaded down on top of him. "That's the story of my life," he said. "I swear to God. A little too late for everything."

"Please get in," she begged him.

Lane turned and started toward the house. "Katie," he called. "Katie, I'm coming. Katie, stay there — I'm coming, Katie."

He stumbled near the front gate, then picked himself up, walked toward the sagging front porch and up the stairs. He reached for the doorknob, and the door gave, instantly.

He was in a hospital corridor, the rain dripping from him. He heard muffled bells and announcements on a loudspeaker, and murmuring voices, and then a doctor came over to him. The doctor fiddled nervously with the stethoscope around his neck. His voice was grimly professional, struggling to conjure up a personal sympathy to cover a most impersonal death. "You're ... Mr. Lane?"

Lane nodded. "I came as fast as I could. One of my neighbors told me that —"

He stopped abruptly, seeing the look on the doctor's face.

"I'm afraid you're too late, Mr. Lane. It was pneumonia. We did everything we could but —"

Lane didn't hear anything else.

"You're too late, Mr. Lane." The words flooded his brain, echoing and reechoing, smashing against the walls of his consciousness. Too late. Much too late. And always too late. He was late that bloody dawn in Normandy when the funked-out kid got caught in the hedgerows and he'd lost a race with a German tiger tank, having to throw himself into a ditch at the last moment while the tank turned the kid into a screaming, mincemeat pancake; he was too late telling his father that it was time to slow down, that at age fifty-five-plus, a man had to slow down to a walk. And then his father was dead of a heart attack. And he was too late in his own realization of time passing — much as Tim Riley had failed to note that dingy little bars with sawdust floors were becoming extinct, along with the nickel beer and the free sandwich — and it followed that he was too late in his own awareness that the soft sell, the friendly passing of the time of day, and the honoring of the word of mouth was an ancient salesmanship long since passé. And with Katie — God, how late he'd been. How belated had been his awareness of her frailty, her littleness, and the thin line that separated humans from extinction. Late. Always late. So Goddamned late. Then he closed his eyes and covered his ears against the noise inside his head — because he couldn't take any more. He simply couldn't take any more.

It was an anxious, tight-lipped Jane Alcott who on the following day tried for the fifth time to reach Randy Lane's apartment, only to hear a filtered voice answer, "I'm sorry. Mr. Lane's apartment isn't answering."

"Thank you," she said, putting the phone down. Then she looked up and saw Harvey Doane standing there by her desk.

"I could have saved you the trouble," he said. "Your boss spent the night in the city jail. Little squib in the morning paper."

Behind him Pritikin appeared, carrying his briefcase. He stopped, looked first at Miss Alcott and Doane, then at the closed door of Lane's office.

Doane turned to him, smiling. "Oh, Mr. Pritikin. I'm afraid we're minus a sales director this morning."

If she could hit him with something, Miss Alcott thought. Something heavy on that pompadoured, Edwardian hair — or strangle him with that broad six-inch striped tie.

"Lane's sick?" Pritikin asked, and it was an accusation.

"I would imagine so," Doane chuckled, "after spending the night in a drunk tank!"

There was an ice-cold silence.

"Should you hear from Mr. Lane," Pritikin said to Jane, "tell him I'd like very much to see him at his earliest convenience." Then he continued on into his office.

"Just a small suggestion, Miss Alcott," Doane said to her. "Always play the favorites."

She looked deep into the boyish face and the Vaseline smile. "That applies to thoroughbred horses, Mr. Doane. You happen to be a jackal!"

She wasn't aware of how loud her voice was until she noted the line of secretaries staring at her.

Doane felt almost nauseous with humiliation. He sensed the eyes of the women on him. Then he cleared his throat. "As of the moment, Miss Alcott — *you* are unemployed." But he was conscious that this was a skimpy face-saving item that saved nothing. This bosomy broad had laid him out, and precious damned little could be salvaged. He retreated back into his office, but too late to escape the last salvo.

Miss Alcott had risen and was regarding him steadily. "At last," she said, "I have something to thank you for. Because not to have to work for you, Mr. Doane, is my most cherished ambition."

The double doors at the far end of the corridor opened, and Randy Lane appeared.

Miss Alcott's eyes widened. Doane turned to look in that direction.

Lane looked bearded, disheveled, a little lost as he walked very slowly past the secretaries at their desks, each of whom gave him a little side look and then stared, fascinated, at the tableau of Doane and Alcott. It was a collective holding of breaths, waiting for the Confrontation.

Lane walked past both of them, directly into his office, and closed the door.

"Are you going to tell him?" Doane asked tersely. "Or shall I?"

Miss Alcott stepped out from behind her desk. "You put your hand on that doorknob," she said softly, "and I'll break it off at the wrist."

She waited just long enough to see his face burn red; then she went into Lane's office.

He was standing behind his desk as if waiting for her. "Jesus," he said, "I'm a dull Goddamned man — and I'd count it a favor, Janie ... honest to God I would ... if you didn't look at me sympathetically."

"Okay," she said, "no sympathy. How about a cup of black coffee instead?"

He shook his head. "Add this to my long list of accomplishments. I now have a record of arrest."

"I know," she said.

He squinted, scratched at his beard stubble, and looked a little confused. "You know," he said, "a great deal can happen to a man in twenty-four hours."

Then the phone rang. Lane looked at it briefly, then ignored it. Jane Alcott finally moved over and picked it up. "Mr. Lane's office," she said. She looked worried, covered the mouthpiece. "It's Mr. Pritikin."

He took the receiver from her and sat down in his chair. "Randolph Lane here. Yes, sir, I quite understand. Oh, yes, indeed. I know all about corporate images. That, too, Mr. Pritikin. I know the value of good public relations. Oh, yes, indeed, sir. I'm close to an expert on that. I quite understand. I'll have vacated my desk by —" He stopped, looking at his wristwatch. "Would ten minutes be okay? Fine. And thank you for telling me."

He put the receiver down, pointed at her. "No sympathy. You promised."

"No sympathy," she repeated, the sharp, yearning hunger for him twisting at her insides.

He stood up, opened up a couple of desk drawers, fumbled around and picked up nothing except the bottle of half-consumed whiskey. He cradled this under his arm like a football and then picked up his wife's picture. "I don't think there's anything else around here," he said, looking around the room, "that belongs to me or that I want to take with me. When you do your housecleaning for Mr. Doane — if you should run across anything, just —"

She cut in. "I won't be working for Mr. Doane — or anyone else around here. Wherever you go — that's where I go."

He looked at her a little enigmatically. "That's biblical," he said, "and it's very sweet." He shook his head. "But I'm afraid that won't be possible. Where I'm going, Jane, I don't think they'd let you in."

He laughed a little as he came out from behind his desk and moved toward the door. He turned to her. "Good-bye, Janie, dear. I've been late ... too late all my life. Now I'm going to go back and stake a claim to some of the better moments. And this trip ... I'll be a son of a bitch if I'll be late for this one!"

He left the office and moved down the row of secretaries' desks, conscious of their staring at him but not giving a damn about them or anything else. When he passed the switchboard operator, she called out to him. "There's a call for you, Mr. Lane."

Lane leaned over the little partition separating the switchboard area, picked up a phone. "Mr. Lane no longer works here," he said, "and Mr. Lane no longer lives here. And Mr. Lane is no longer available. And if you're interested in plastics ... I recommend a Mr. Harvey Doane. He is of the new breed ... and should you not know it ... the new breed is built out of plastics!"

He put the phone down and moved out of the office, announcing over his shoulder to the gaping switchboard operator: "If anybody should ask ... I've gone to a homecoming at Tim Riley's Bar. *My homecoming.*"

Mr. Pritikin sat at his desk and was surprised and not very pleased when Miss Alcott entered his office, unannounced. She stood a few feet from his desk, and he noticed that she looked very pale. "What is —" he began to say, and then shut up.

"For Mr. Randolph Lane," Jane Alcott said, "who has just departed the premises. One small lonely word on his behalf. Since nobody else seems to give a damn. In exchange for twenty-five pretty good years, you've given him the boot and the back of your hand. Now he's alone and tired and a little frightened. Maybe the least you could have given him, Mr. Pritikin, would have been a gold watch. That wouldn't have been bad. But just a ... a word ... a gentle word would have been better. Just a reminder to him that he's not obsolete. He's not unloved. He's not a relic to be carted off to the dump. Now he's chasing ghosts ... when all he really needed was that one word to tell him that he had *worth*. That much you could have given him."

She stood there silently for a moment, her head down; then she looked up. "That much, Mr. Pritikin," she said very gently, "*you should have given him!*"

Before he could answer, she had turned and left the office.

When Randy Lane finally reached Tim Riley's Bar much later that night, two hard-hatted construction workers were just taking the front door off its hinges and carrying it out to a truck parked out front. Two other men inside were removing the last of the electrical fixtures. The truck's lights had been left on to give illumination to the scene.

Lane stepped through the opening to the bar and almost ran into one of the hardhats as he walked past Lane carrying two rolls of wire.

"What's going on?" Lane asked.

"What the hell does it look like?" the workman answered, without stopping. "We're knocking the place down."

"Tonight?" Lane called to him through the opening.

"Overtime," the workman said from the sidewalk as he headed toward the truck. "We're behind schedule. You wanna get out of the way, mister?"

Other workmen went in and out past Lane. There was the sound of a pneumatic drill from another section of the ground floor, and outside another work crew went industriously at the job of knocking down the walls. One of them had gone behind the bar and was starting to hammer at the big mirror that hung behind it.

"Wait a minute," Lane called to him, running towards the bar. "Wait a minute."

He vaulted the bar, seized the man, and whirled him around.

He was looking into the face of Tim Riley, and suddenly the lights were on.

There was a red-white-and-blue bunting stretched across the bar. "Welcome Home, Randy." The booths were filled. The jukebox was playing in competition with the piano. People walked back and forth with beer mugs in their hands, laughing and singing.

And then he saw his father at the piano and walked over to him; his father, with the barbed-wire white hair that stuck straight up, and the perpetual grin, and the kindly wrinkled blue eyes. His father winked at him. "How are you, Randy?"

"Fine, Pop," Lane answered, "just fine." Then he turned and saw Katie. He held out his hands to her, and she approached him. He took her to him, holding her very closely and very tightly, kissing her hair.

"Hello, darling," she said to him.

"Katie," Lane answered hoarsely. "Katie ... God, how I've missed you —"

Tim Riley came out from behind the bar and walked over to Lane, slapping him on the back. "Good to see you, Tim," Lane said. "Awful good to see you."

"And you, Randy — good to see you. What's more, it's on the house!" He beckoned to an aproned waiter, who drew a beer and slid it expertly down the bar. Tim caught it deftly and handed it over to Lane.

Then Lane's father began to play "It's a Long Way to Tipperary" on the piano and the crowd began to move in around them. Lane looked at the faces. He knew them. Pete Denovitch — dead of a heart attack in '54. Played ball with him on the school football team. And there was his wife. They called her Brownie. A tiny woman, barely five feet tall. And there was McDonough, his stiff policeman's tunic opened up with an undershirt showing through. He knew them all. Their names, where they lived, what they meant to him.

He put his arm around Katie and kept looking at her profile, holding tight to her, touching her, caressing her, and every now and then leaning down to kiss her.

Then all the people faced Lane and held up their beer mugs. After a moment their voices died away and all was silent. It was then that Katie very softly began to sing "Auld Lang Syne," and then a chorus of soft voices joined her.

Lane turned her to him, staring into her face, which somehow seemed shadowed — the features hazy. "Katie," Lane said, "no sad songs for this occasion. This is a homecoming!"

From someplace far off he heard a wall crumble and a glass break, then the sound of the pneumatic drill.

"Go ahead, Katie," Lane said louder, "sing." He looked around the group. "All of you — sing. This is an occasion. I mean ... it's not every day a guy comes back." His voice was louder and more supplicating. "Please ... everybody sing!"

His father stopped playing the piano and turned to look at him. "Randy," he said softly.

"Go ahead, Pop. Give us a couple of choruses of 'Tipperary.' Go ahead, Tim — play the piano for him." He whirled around to face the crowd. "Everybody ... everybody sing!"

Glass was being shattered and plaster cracked and wood splintered, and then all noise stopped for the second time. Again it was absolutely still.

"How 'bout that, Randy," his father said to him. "They're tearing down Tim Riley's Bar." He looked over to Tim. "That's what they're doing, Tim."

Riley nodded.

"Don't pay any attention!" Lane shouted. "Forget about them! Come on, everybody. This is where it is — right here. This place. This bar."

They just stared at him.

He grabbed Katie. "I'm back, Katie. Understand? It's 1945 and I'm back. We're going to get married. You and me. Then we're going to buy a white two-story house. That's what's going to happen. But let me tell you something ... let me tell you *this* right now ... we're going change everything. We're going to do it right this time. I'm not going to lose you, Katie."

He clutched at her as if by this embrace he could put off death and everything else. "I'm not going to lose you, Katie. I swear to God. I'm not going to lose you —"

The lights began to fade and the figures became even more indistinct.

Lane moved away from Katie and reached for one person after the other and felt nothing. He went from face to face, figure to figure, then back to his father, reaching for him. "Pop," he said, "please ... Pop."

There was just stillness. "Wait a minute ... all of you," he said to the figures as they disappeared in front of him. "I can't stay here. I don't have any place. I'm an antique ... a has-been. I don't have any function here. I don't have any purpose."

He held out his hands in front of him, fists clenched. "You leave me now and I'm marooned!" He pointed toward the window. "I can't survive out there! Pop? Tim? They stacked the deck that way. They fix it so you get elbowed off the earth! You just don't understand what's going on now! The whole bloody world is coming apart at the seams. And I can't hack it." He began to sob. "I swear to God ... I can't hack it."

He turned, and there was Katie alongside. "Katie," said brokenly, "you're all I've got. I can't lose you ... I've lost everything else."

And then he was alone save for a workman who had reentered the room. He looked out toward what was once a wall and saw the parking lot alongside. "Jesus, buddy," the workman said, "you wanna get yourself killed? Get the hell out of here. The whole place is gonna collapse in a minute. Now, come on," he ordered, pulling Lane's arm.

Lane found himself out on the sidewalk. The workmen had put up a cordon of rope, and there were several sidewalk superintendents who had gathered to see the final destruction — the last three walls cave in. But Randy Lane didn't wait. He walked away from the place, willing to himself that he wouldn't hear the noise. He wouldn't hear the walls come down. He wanted nothing but silence for the rest of the night. But as he approached the corner he heard something else. There were voices singing "For He's a Jolly Good Fellow."

He stopped abruptly and looked across the street. There was the cocktail lounge, all lit up. And there were faces at the window. He recognized Pritikin and he also saw Jane Alcott as she moved away from the window and came out the door to walk over to him. She held out her hand, and he took it and followed her.

She led him inside the cocktail lounge. It was crowded with people. He noticed Officer McDonough and a few other of the older men he'd worked with over the years.

Then Pritikin detached himself from a group and approached him. "Randy Lane," he said in a voice Lane had never heard before. "It occurred to some of us ... your friends ... that a man shouldn't have twenty-five years go by without being remembered ... and thanked ... and reminded that he is held in deep affection and sizeable esteem."

Outside there was the distant noise of a wall collapsing.

"It's to my discredit, Randy, and I ask you to forgive me for not having told you this before ... and more than once." He raised his glass. "To the past twenty-five years, Mr. Lane, but much more important ... to the next twenty-five."

Jane Alcott kissed him on the side of his face. Another man shook his hand. Even Harvey Doane, looking mortally wounded, tossed him a salute from a bar stool.

Outside another wall collapsed; then somebody handed Lane a glass, and Miss Alcott hugged him and they began to sing "For He's a Jolly Good Fellow."

Outside there was no more Tim Riley's Bar. Dust was just settling over the broken walls, the mounds of brick, the slabs of glass. Only the bar remained, gouged and bent. But from this wreckage came the soft sound of "Auld Lang Syne" sung by other voices.

A workman threw a battered sign into the back of the truck, then shut the tailgate. The sign read "Tim Riley's Bar." It rested atop a pile of two-by-fours and a couple of legless chairs. But it was the only thing that could be seen over the sides of the truck, like the forlorn banner of a defeated army.

The truck pulled away and carried "Tim Riley's Bar" with it.

And Randy Lane sipped at his beer and looked at the truck as it went by. Then he looked down into the scrubbed, shining face of Jane Alcott and noted the freshness, the loveliness, and the giving in the eyes. Not like Katie. Blonde, rather than dark, eyes set farther apart, face just a bit older as he remembered her, but a good face — a lovely face. And he felt something stirring ... something he hadn't felt in a long time.

He smiled at her and put his glass down, then looked at the singing people surrounding him, the ones he'd have to live with and die with for the rest of his time. There was no one else. At long last he realized that.

Made in the USA
San Bernardino, CA
07 December 2016